Outc

OUTCASTS

Badlands Book Three

From The Bestselling Author

Natalie Bennett

Copyright

Outcasts (Badlands Book Three) by Natalie Bennett

Cover Design: Covers By Combs

Editing by: Pinpoint Editing

Dedication

To my Quib.

Thank you for never letting me give up.

Contents

Want to be the first to hear about new releases or sales? Join my newsletter.

www.nataliebennett.net

Follow me on: Facebook-Natalie Bennett/writer

Follow me on: Instagram-Authornataliebennett

Join my Reader's group:-Natalie's Nefarious Readers

Upcoming Books 2018

King Of Hearts-6.09

Ace Of Spades-6.22

Heathens-TBA

Fuck Toy-7.01

Devils With Halos-TBA

Other books by Natalie Bennett

UltraViolence Duet

UltraViolence

Blue Velvet

Obscene Trilogy

Love Obscene

Love Corrupted

Love Depraved–10/31

Badlands Series

Savages

Deviants

Outcasts

Heathens

Degenerates *The next generation*

Standalones

Mercy: A Dark Erotica

Rose De Muerte

Pernicious Red

Fuck Toy

Playlist

Spotify

Gin Wigamore- Black Sheep

NF-10 Feet Down

NF-Mansion

BHM-Can You Feel My Heart?

Trevor Moran-Sinner

Coldplay- Fix You

Lacey Strum-Rot

The Neighborhood-Heaven

Disturbed-Down With The Sickness

5FDP-The Devil's Own

The Fray- Never Say Never

Stone Sour- Song #3

Tove Lo- Moments

Halestorm- The Reckoning

Fall Out Boy- Bishops Knife Trick

Three Days Grace- The High Road

Three Days Grace-Painkiller

Three Days Grace- Animal I Have Become

Natalie Bennett

Wasteland- 10 Years

Evanescence- Imperfection

Shinedown- Cut The Cord

Sam Smith- Life Support

Niykee Heaton-Lullaby

Halsey-Gasoline

Halsey-Roman Holiday

PVRIS-Separate

PVRIS-Fire

The Weekend-Pray For Me

Breaking Benjamin-Red Cold River

Breaking Benjamin-Save Yourself

Breaking Benjamin-The Dark Of You

In This Moment-Sick Like Me

In This Moment-Forever

AUTHOR'S NOTE

Warning: Graphic Content

Outcasts is the **third** book in a dark erotic series with an underlying dystopian tone. You can read this as a standalone but I highly recommend reading Savages and Deviants before proceeding.

I have done a recap on the next page that contains spoilers for those who have not read the first and second book.

Please know your limitations. This series is full of vulgar language. If you have issues reading about very dark and depraved themes with zero regard for moral boundaries, this is not the series for you. If you want questions with simple and easy to find answers, redeeming heroes, and a guaranteed happily ever after, I'm not the author for you. **This is not a fluffy romance.**

Recap

This is a quick rundown of events from Savages and Deviants that will pertain to Outcasts. Mild **spoilers** are ahead for anyone who has not read the first two books.

Cali saved Arlen from a barn where she was being held by cannibals. They were both taken in by Romero, the leader of the Savages, a satanic cult masquerading as a lawless gang. He was accompanied by two men when this happened: Cobra and Grimm.

The first two books were mainly about disbanding another cult known as The Order, which was ultimately achieved. In the first book, there was a room full of people's belongings. That will be explained in more detail. Arlen has since been kidnapped by Romero's brother Noah as 'collateral'.

Just remember to keep in mind as you read Outcasts that nothing can ever be taken at face value.

This book is a standalone in the series and centers around Arlen and Grimm—aptly nicknamed after the Grim Reaper.

I hope you love these two crazies as much as I do. ☺

pulvis et umbra sumus.

Prelude

There is no light to be found here, only darkness.

Our world is full of monsters that no longer bother wearing friendly faces.

The saints and the uncorrupted have either perished or hidden away. Sinners and the dearly depraved have gladly taken their place.

I am not an exception.

Outcasts

I am a lover of death.

It came to me in the form of a man revered as the Grim Reaper himself. They call him a demon, something straight out of nightmares; a loyal solider in the devil's army.

He was the reckoning I never saw coming.

I am the Persephone to his Hades.

He is the misery I crave.

He became my absolution by showing me that hell, too, had beauty.

I became his salvation by accepting him for who and what he was.

We are not soul-mates, but one eternal flame split in two.

We were going to set fire to anything and anyone that stood between us and the way back to our dark paradise.

Our story is passionate, sometimes painful, other times brutal.

I advise you leave your morals at the door.

You will find we outcasts have none.

Chapter One

PAST

Arlen

He told me to sit taller, look softer, keep my mouth shut, and smile.

Clearly, he forgot who his daughter was. I *never* shut the hell up. My mouth was a pistol, my tongue a silver bullet. I wasn't particularly good at aimin, but I could aim just fine when backed into a corner.

It wasn't the best trait to have, but it'd come in handy quite a few times.

I figured this'd be one of em.

“I’m not marryin this man.” I cut right into the conversation, no holds barred.

The room grew so quiet you could hear the leaves swaying on our golden wattle tree in the front yard. My ma shot me a warning look, which I ignored.

“Arlen,” Dad chastised.

“You told me she understood,” Rodrick, the groom in question, sighed.

“I understand just fine, Dick. I’m not marryin you. How about findin a woman closer to your own age?”

See, I thought this was a great suggestion. Dick didn’t. He scoffed, but couldn’t open his mouth to dispute me. At thirty-nine, Rodrick (Dick) was a fairly attractive man, with swoopy blonde hair and money green eyes.

He was also two decades older than me, and the furthest thing from my type. I didn’t really have a type, actually, but if I did, it wasn’t a man in a suit who ate garlic bread with a fork.

That wasn't normal.

My ma rubbed her brow, diverting her gaze as if I'd just sat the weight of the whole damn world on her over-privileged shoulders.

"Why don't we move this discussion into the den?" Dad was already standing to do just that before Rodrick could agree or disagree, shooting me a scathing glare that spoke volumes.

Dad didn't hit; he used words. He told me I'd be no good to anyone bruised up and skittish, so he would break me in another way, like I was a damn colt or somethin. I could tell the last thing Dick wanted to do was go off and have a conversation with him, but he followed regardless.

They left behind their pipin hot lasagna. I wanted to yell after them that there were families who would (literally) strip the tanned flesh from their bodies for the same indulgence.

Hell, some families would eat it, too.

"Arlen, you cannot ruin this deal," Ma hissed the second she heard the door click shut. I whipped back around and shook my head at her.

I studied her from across the table and frowned. She was always so put together. I didn't understand how she could wear those long thin heels all hours of the day, every day. And she never let her hair down. I wish she laughed like she used to. She'd changed so much over the years. Her main goal was being the best wife–the best cook–and the best hostess.

She forgot how to be my mother.

The opinions of strangers held too much weight in this household. I learned to quit caring long ago. I didn't give a rat's ass what anyone thought of me. Ma had been like that once, but now she was stuck.

I could grab her by the shoulders and preach about old times till I was blue in the face; I knew it wouldn't change a thing.

"You hear what you just said? A deal, Momma. You want my marriage to be a *deal*?"

"Sweetheart, she's gone now, and it's important to maintain a healthy working relationship between your father and Rodrick."

"You mean Be—"

"You know you're not to say that name," she interjected.

"Beth. Her *name* is Beth, and she's *your* daughter."

"*Was* my daughter, until she brought shame on this family by running off like some hoodlum in the middle of the night. It's only natural the responsibility move to you.

"Rodrick wants to ensure he has an in with the wealthiest family in Centriole before he agrees to your father's terms. You know how hard he works to hold his position."

I had to refrain from rollin my eyes. I'd heard the 'dad works hard speech' so many times I could recite it in my sleep.

What he did that was so strenuous was beyond my understanding.

Seemed to me he got dressed up every day just to sit on his ass and make phone calls so everyone else had to work for a livin.

Attempting to tuck a strand of hair behind my ear, I grunted when I remembered it was already pinned back in some extra fancy hairdo Ma insisted on.

"Maybe you should tell me what this big deal is, if it's that important."

"You know I can't do that."

What was with all the secrecy?

"I'm not sure if this is the part where I say we're ahead of such times, or times are chagin, since no one around here seems inclined to give me a history lesson."

She sighed—dramatically, I might add—but I still didn't get any real explanation. I never did.

"Dick's meant to be marryin my sister. That's probably why she left in the first place.

It don't matter now though, does it? Ya'll won't give me the option of makin my own choices"

When she let out her signature musical laugh, I knew exactly where this conversation was goin.

"Your choices have resulted in all those tattoos covering your body in a poor attempt to rebel, screwing the pool boy, and failing every aspect of etiquette—your speech, especially."

There was no reasoning with this woman. I was tired of wastin my time trying to explain who I was to someone committed to misunderstanding me.

How many times did I have to tell her the ink on my body was art? That the pool boy had an actual name, and was my first of everything.

"You keep trying to change me into everything he hates."

Her swallow was audible, and suddenly she had a bit of invisible lint on her skirt.

The *he* in question was another subject I was not to discuss—a lesson drilled into my skull from the time I was nine years old.

"You could be happy," she solemnly deflected.

I huffed in defeat. We always ended up back at this, forever talking in circles.

"Where are you going?" she asked as I pushed away from the table and stood up.

"Goin to wash this gunk off my face, and then I'm goin to bed."

"Your father will want to speak with you."

She knew full well I wasn't going to wait around for *that* conversation.

I made my way to my room and, once inside, immediately headed for the bathroom.

I laughed at my reflection the second I saw it. I looked like a walking scuff mark.

Ma had wanted to hide some of my tattoos and lathered me in some sort of cover up. It was a hot mess, and extra pointless.

I'd been the subject of gossip and ridicule for years. Everyone in this judgmental city knew I was inked.

I removed the pins from my hair and ran my fingers through the long wavy strands to give it back some life. The few lighter highlights I'd been permitted to have boldly contrasted with the natural dark brown.

Letting the hideously dull teacup dress billow to the bathroom floor, I took a quick shower, and threw on my plaid pajama shorts and an old metal t-shirt, instantly feeling much more like myself.

After shutting the lights off, I turned the lever on the window to let some fresh air in, and settled beneath my abstract comforter. I rolled onto my side, and stared out at the pretty night sky, where the moon sat by her lonesome.

Our backyard seemed to stretch on forever, ending where a solid brick wall wrapped around Centriole as a whole began.

I felt trapped here in every way. I knew Ma loved me, and I liked to imagine Dad did too, but they would never accept me as I was.

It hurt that I couldn't be what they needed, and it hurt I couldn't be what I wanted. I was fed and watered daily, but something told me there was more to life than this. My cage may have had bars of gleaming gold, but it was still a cage.

Many referred to this place as The Kingdom, a utopia of sorts. I could understand why, but that's not how I saw it.

Our grass was lime green, the water was a shimmering blue, our stores were stocked with food, and people could safely go for walks in the middle of the night, knowing the wall was constantly being patrolled. You could even score some happy pills, if that was your thing.

On the other side of the wall was the affront to my morbid curiosity.

The Badlands: a prettied up hostile desert wasteland.

The pinkish plains were home to various gangs of undesirables and an enclave of cannibals.

I suppose that was the purpose of the wall in the first place: to keep 'them' out. The deviants and outliers: people deemed not good enough to live among us. Outcasts. Those rejected by society.

I couldn't help wonderin how vastly different their lives was from mine, reckoning I was the only person in the whole city who wanted to know what life would be like outside that eyesore of a damn wall. It wasn't like I'd never asked someone these questions neither. I had—many times. No one ever gave me a real answer. Just like ma wouldn't share any knowledge of history with me.

Thinkin of the loaded up duffel bag stowed beneath my bed, I knew I'd be leavin this place behind sooner than later, and Ma and dad ain't have the slightest clue. Nobody did but the man that shared my secret with me.

My reputation has never preceded me.

To anyone outside looking in, I was Arlen Prosner—spoiled rich bitch that did everything her daddy told her.

None of that was remotely true.

That girl would have never considered her uncle's whispered offer to leave The Kingdom in two weeks time.

I knew once we left, we wasn't goin ever return. Coming back meant going through a lengthy process, and most were immediately shot or turned away. There were two ways in and out of the city, both heavily guarded. No one was forced to stay in, but once you got beyond a certain point…that was it.

There were even signs posted; I'd memorized them by heart.

Warning: Beyond this fence is no longer the territory of Centriole. Thereafter no person within the territory beyond this fence is a resident of our city or shall be acknowledged, recognized, or protected by the governing body therein.

You are now entering the Badlands.

Good luck.

It was debatable if the 'good luck' was genuine or not, but I had questions, a wayward sister, burnin curiosity, and an itch to break free.

Even knowing what was out there, how dangerous and foolish the choice would seem to anyone else, I was goin.

When I looked at the Badlands from the comfort of my bedroom, I didn't see mutilated bodies or a war brewin between two powerful men.

What I saw was the lack of a wall, freedom from a life of being a Stepford wife, and popping out babies for a man twice my age.

I didn't see how damn naïve I was.

I didn't see myself befriending a tiny blonde who was a full blown psycho beneath her flawless exterior. I never foresaw the path my life would take from that day forward.

I made a life changin decision, and I ain't have the foresight to see how drastic it would be.

Outcasts

I could have never foreseen all the ways I was goin to suffer on a precipice of insanity, before death finally gave me peace.

Chapter Two

<u>Present</u>

Arlen

Red wine scented breath was on my neck. There was pressure between my legs and a weight on my chest.

Lucidity washed over me and I knew I'd been drugged again. The stiff mattress beneath me barely creaked as he thrust in and out. Raw. He was always raw when he forced his cock inside me when I couldn't give consent. My fingers twitched as my body became as awake as my brain.

I did my best to ignore his groans of pleasure, feeling the acid bubblin in my stomach as I had no choice but to lie wide open. I felt like a starfish, sticky and stuck.

Willing all feeling to come back, I flexed both fists as a test, reacting before it had fully sunken in that I could move.

"Get the fuck off me, Noah!"

So caught up in releasing the pleasure in his tiny balls, he hadn't realized I was awake. His face was the perfect picture of surprise as he fell onto the floor, leaving behind a nausea-inducing wetness between my thighs.

"I was almost done," he sighed, as if I'd majorly inconvenienced him, already grabbing for the Cattle prod I could never get to in time.

"You're a sick fuck!" I closed my legs and sat up, preparing to fight him off best I could if he tried comin at me again.

I wouldn't rush him. I'd learned my lesson the first and second time he'd shocked me with the damn stick in his hand—the one he acquired after he had to have me pulled off him. The first time we fought, we were like two men in a ring goin for a championship belt. His precious ego hadn't taken that loss too well.

That's when the prod came into the picture. He'd blindsided me with it, shocked the hell outta me and brought me clean to my knees. I never wanted to be on the business end of that thing again.

If I ever got a hold of it, I was gonna jam it straight up his ass and fry his shitter from the inside out.

"Petals, I don't know why you deny what's between us."

"Ain't anything between us, you sick, shrivel dicked asshole." I glared at him. He shut his eyes and sighed, tightening his grip on the prod. You'd think I would've learned to shut the hell up, considerin my mouth is what got me in this situation.

"Petals." He sighed again.

I curled my lip at the stupid name. Why the hell did he choose it?

He muttered something unintelligible beneath his breath, and wordlessly readjusted the ridiculous white robe he always wore. His father's order had been disbanded, largely thanks to him, so I didn't see his point at first, but after being stuck with him for so long I'd overheard quite a few things I shouldn't have.

"Denial can only hold out for so long. You know you're not leaving me, so you might as well make the best of our relationship."

He stared at me expectantly, and I stared back in pure disgust.

I *hated* him. Not just for what he did to me, but what he'd done to Cali, too, the sweet girl who was supposed to be his sister, turned out she wasn't, but that was still damn sickening.

I *hated* him touching me the way he did. I *hated* this feelin of helplessness.

"You're pathetic. Get out of my room."

Swiping a hand through his short, dark hair, he frowned and gave a shake of his head. He looked nothing like Romero, his brother. And they couldn't have been more different.

One was a rat placed in a maze and made to do another's bidding, while the other was the head of the Savages. Romero was a king, the very devil I'd heard so much about, and the Badlands was his personal hell.

After a brief hiatus, he was back, and making that known to everyone and anyone who tested him with my newfound best friend, Cali, at his side.

Noah desperately coveted the power Romero had. He wanted the adoration and loyalty his brother's acolytes willingly gave.

He would never have it. What was it with men in their need to have big ol dick measurin contests? Noah was strong, but debilitated next to Romero. He was occasionally smart; Romero was ten times smarter.

None of that had stopped his thirst for his brother's throne, and that, in its self, made him a damn fool.

Not to mention the army that stood between him and making that happen, and the other key players he'd have to go up against. Last time I pointed all that out, he almost punched my head off my shoulders. Lesson learned.

"I've been trying to make it work between us for the past three weeks. I don't know what else to do." He went to the door, keeping his front towards me so I couldn't jump him from behind, the prod out in front of him like a shield. "You'll change your mind by Thursday morning."

The door was open and shut with him on the other side before I could ask what he meant. I didn't even know what day it was.

One lock clicked, followed by the second, and then finally, the chain was slid in place.

As soon as his footsteps faded, I was off the bed like a fire had been lit beneath my ass, straight into the lemon scented bathroom.

It was tiny with dull yellow tiled flooring, and only contained a toilet and sink, but all I needed was running water and a bar of soap.

Turning the little silver knob with an H embellished on the top, I grabbed one of my wash rags from the wicker basket Noah had placed on the toilet's tank.

Steam rose from the stream of water. I drenched the rag, fighting the urge to pull my hand back even as it shook uncontrollably from nerves and turned a dark pink from the heat. My heart was beating so fast, I thought for sure it was going to come right through my chest.

"Ignore it all," I whispered to myself.

I rolled my lips together in a firm line to keep the hysteria ready to empty from my lungs quiet. I'd cried too many times already—ugly, terribly loud sobs.

I wouldn't give him any more of my tears. I couldn't, anyway; the pain was there, but the well had run empty.

I never let Noah see how severely his actions sabotaged my psyche.

It excited him and made things worse for me. I'd yet to decide if it was a small saving grace when he raped me and I awoke to feel nothing but the come and soreness he left behind, or a disadvantage not to feel everything from the beginning.

There were times I woke up. Others, I didn't. Often enough, he woke me up for the pure entertainment of fighting his way inside me. I'd been taken advantage of so many times at this point, I wasn't sure it mattered anymore. I just wanted it to stop.

I'd never felt more trapped than I did now, and sometimes I thought I deserved this.

I was the one who ran away from home, so desperate for a taste of freedom.

Watching my uncle be cut open and dismembered for a family of cannibals' weekly supper wasn't penance enough.

I didn't miss the city, though—not even a little bit.

I suppose life was now punishing me for the company I chose to keep. She was a mean bitch like that.

Grabbing the soap and making good use of the rag, I began to vigorously scrub between my legs, ignoring how badly it burned. I had half a mind to shove the soap inside me to clean away where he'd been.

I was so damn grateful his intent wasn't to get me pregnant. He made me take a contraceptive with the only drink he allowed me to have—water.

It was always a gamble if he'd laced it or not, but it was either risk pregnancy by refusing the liquid, or drink it to receive the pill.

I was real familiar with the package it came in. My ma made me take the same ones.

As far as I knew, they were only available in Centriole. To get something like that in the Badlands, you would need a pretty penny or solid connection. The fact that Noah had some told me more than he might have thought.

That kind of thing is what made him so stupid. He had loose lips, and never seemed to realize I heard everything that went on when I wasn't drugged. Didn't he know I was foe, not friend?

I retained as much information as I could because I still had a small sliver of hope I'd be gettin out of this shithole. I knew if it were up to Cali, she'd have stormed the building with a take no prisoners approach already, but she wasn't in any position to do that. She was growing a baby.

She may not have been some mushy sentimental person, but I knew she wouldn't risk her child—nor would Romero ever allow it. Not for me. And I didn't want her to. She was Romero's queen—quite literally.

The man had a nasty attitude and seemed made of stone, but he adored her. I was envious of that. I didn't think epic love was in the cards for me, though.

The only person I'd ever felt drawn to like a magnet wasn't really a relationship kinda guy, and there was a whole unrequited mess between us.

Shutting the sink off, I wrung out my rag, avoiding my reflection. I didn't want to see the shame looking back at me. After re-positioning my slip—the only clothing Noah allowed—I went back into the bedroom.

The four wood paneled walls were different than the teal ones that had surrounded me a month ago.

According to what Noah had just said, we'd been here three weeks, which meant we'd be moving again soon. He never stayed in the same place for long. I had no real measurement of time in regards to how long he'd had me, but I estimated a solid sixty days, minimum.

Crawling onto the bed, I avoided the place my legs had just been sprawled apart. I drew my knees to my chest, and rested my cheek on them, staring at nothing.

The room was barren, aside from the bed and a small round coffee table.

The only window had a thick piece of plywood across it to prevent me from escaping or seeing out—probably both.

I sat there in that dimly lit cell with nothing to distract me. I sat there for minutes, hours, maybe even days, and with nothing to busy myself with, my mind ran wild. I never knew silence could be so loud.

I missed my friends.

And I missed *him*.

I missed my shadow, the reaper at my back who watched over me without wanting anything in return. I could make myself blissfully and deliriously numb to my surroundings if I filled my every thought with nothing but Grimm.

If I saw him in a dream, he was always torn away when I woke again, and I was never ready to say goodbye.

I'd honestly expected him to come for me out of everyone else, but he hadn't shown up yet.

Noah's ominous taunt became the focal point of a slow growing paranoia. I had no idea what he had planned for me. I wasn't adept at dealing with things like this.

I told myself to think positive thoughts, but the hope I kept a firm grasp on was beginning to slip through my fingers.

Chapter Three

Arlen

Nothing tragic happened that morning.

I woke from the sound of the door clicking shut with heavy sleep in my eyes from fighting it off for so long. A silver tray with oatmeal and a fruit cup sat waiting for me on the coffee table—another regularity, and my only breakfast option.

Noon came around, bringing me closer to whatever it was Noah wanted. I was able to pretend all was fine for a few minutes as I brushed my teeth and hair.

My actions may have seemed pointless, but I knew I needed to eat for my own well-being, and keeping somewhat clean was my way of refusing to fall apart completely.

I guess you could say it was a façade.

As soon as I was done, I was left with the same problem I always had: nothing to do but sit on my ass and wonder what was gonna happen next. I leaned back on the bed, listening to the movement throughout the house we were holed up in.

I heard multiple voices, but that was nothing new. I theorized all the possible scenarios as to what Noah could be up to in the long run, but continued to pull a blank.

Keeping me was strange in itself. He knew who I was, and made no effort to contact my father for a ransom or power exchange. He'd once said I was his collateral, a reason for Romero not to hunt him down, but that didn't explain much, either.

We both knew if his brother wanted him dead, he'd be dead.

With no way of knowing what time it was, I tried to use basic math as a timetable for when the sun traded places with the moon. Still, nothing happened—not right away, anyway.

I was half-asleep when they showed up; four men I'd never seen strolled into the room with Noah right behind them.

My danger radar immediately went through the roof, as did the tempo of my pulse. I could nearly feel it in my throat. All of em had on the usual dark jeans and dark shirts men in the Badlands wore, but they were too rough around the edges to be anyone Noah regularly associated with.

"What is this?" I asked, sitting a little taller and pressing my back flat against the worn headboard.

"Petals, these are my new friends," Noah announced, making his way to the front of the little group, prod in his hand.

"We both know damn well you don't have any friends. Cut the shit and tell me what's really goin on."

Two of the men laughed at my accurate assumption, while the biggest one gave me a smile full of surprisingly white teeth. That's what I got for jumping to conclusions.

He looked rugged.

Looking at him a little closer, I took notice of the tattoo on his neck—a V with a black snake intertwined around it. I also realized he was much older than I was, but his overall hygiene didn't seem bad.

None of that explained why they were in the room with me. I looked at their faces, and suddenly had an inkling of where this was going.

Their aura was menacing.

The way they were lookin at me was as if they were starving and had just found a five-course meal.

"You definitely don't look like any Kingdom bitch we've ever seen," one of them commented, dropping his heated gaze to where my nipples were easily seen through the white fabric of my slip.

My stomach knotted in a million different directions, and a dull ache resonated through my entire body. I felt like one of the raccoons Dad used to catch in tiny metal traps. I had no way of escaping; I was stuck with danger staring me straight in the face.

"Why are they here?" I asked Noah directly, ignoring the quad.

He opened his mouth to answer but the man who smiled at me held up a hand, shutting him up.

"Arlen, my name's Vance. This is my brother Rex, and these are our boys, Hawke and Vitus."

He aimed a thumb at each of them without taking his eyes off me. Him knowing my name wasn't the least bit surprising.

Anyone who paid enough attention to any form of press knew I was the Regent—or, as he liked to call himself lately, *Mayor*—of Centriole's daughter.

"What do you want with me?"

"Well, I asked Noah here to show me he could make good on his word."

At my blank stare, he chuckled amusedly and partially turned to clamp the man he'd called Vitus on the shoulder and pull him forward.

"It's my boy's twenty-fifth birthday, and Noah promised some exclusive one-on-one time between you two during a round of cards the other night."

"I'm not his to promise." I glared at Vitus. If he was really twenty-five, that sat him only six years older than me, but I could tell just by looking at him that whatever happened in his daily life had matured and hardened him beyond his age.

He had dark curly hair and a solid build. He stared me down with odd bluish-green eyes, one side of his mouth lifting into a grin when I scowled.

"Alright, everybody get out." His gruff demand was met with laughs from everyone but Noah, who had the audacity to look slightly concerned.

Nonetheless, he wordlessly trailed after the others as they filed out of the room, leaving me alone to fend for myself.

"You know, you're a lot prettier in person," he said , inching closer to the bed.

I edged away, wanting him nowhere near me.

My voice may have remained steady, and I could bravely look these men in the eye without crumbling to pieces, but that was only because my mouth seemed to move without approval from my brain half the time.

That ridiculous thing called pride wouldn't allow me to beg for mercy.

In all actuality, I was absolutely terrified. Natural fight or flight instinct had my entire body tensing in apprehension of what was to come. "There are plenty of pretty girls you could go and play with. Why pick me?"

"None of those girls *are* you, Arlen."

I scrambled off the bed, keeping as much space between us as I could. Fightin him wasn't the brightest option. That would do nothing but wear me out or get me hurt.

Vitus shook his head and held both his hands up like he was surrendering. He was quick to hold a finger to his lips when I opened my gob to ask what the hell he was doing.

He continued moving towards me in the same pose, giving a slight shake of his head when I side eyed the bathroom, easily understanding my intent. I took two steps back but didn't have room to go further because of the wall.

"Listen, forcing women to spread their legs isn't my forte, and I don't want to today, but my pops won't be very happy if I walk outta here without getting what we came all this way for," he whispered lowly, stopping an arm's reach away from me.

"How's that my problem? That seems more like a personal issue."

"It's actually just an issue for you. I'm trying to do the right thing. They're outside that door, listening, so you can get on that bed and willingly lie on your back for me, or I can do things the hard way for both of us."

What type of compromise was that? He was getting what he wanted either way. My only options were to fight and ultimately lose—maybe I'd miraculously hand him his ass, but then still have to deal with his posse on the other side of the door—or, I could steel my spine and take it.

There was really only one logical route to go: throwing the battle but still holding out for winning the war.

With a sharp jerk of my chin, I stormed past him and went back to the bed.

I refused to look at him as I laid flat on my back and spread my legs, willing him to just get it over with.

Ma told me being with a man never lasted very long. She'd been trying to prep me for the marriage I didn't want. I'm sure she never imagined her advice would be used for something like this.

It didn't take Vitus long to make a move. The sound of his belt jingling had my hands balling into fists by my sides. I focused on the paint peeling off the ceiling, squeezing my eyes shut when the bed dipped.

Everything inside me resented this, made me hate myself a little more.

I flinched when he placed a hand on my knee.

"It's alright," he cooed, settling between my legs. "I don't need any more Vitus Jrs. running around. Noah told me you're on the pill, though if I had you to breed I can't say I'd complain. I'm clean, by the way." He laughed a little, and my stomach pitched.

This asshole just said 'breed'. I'd never heard any man say that before, and I could wager I knew some damn shitty men. The Savages didn't even do such a thing.

It was a knockout right to the face when I realized the devil and his unholy family had more morals than common men.

There was a brief moment when nothing happened, but then I felt the bareness of firm pectorals.

Something rattled in my chest as my brain screamed at me to do something and stop this from happening.

Smashing my lips into a firm line, I tried to swallow the sob rising up, leaving some garbled sound to slip out in its place.

"Shh, it's okay," he soothed, running a thumb over my hairline. I wanted him to stop sayin that. This was not okay. It would *never* be okay. *I* was never going to be okay.

A second later, he was pushing inside me, forcing his cock in past the dryness.

He continued to whisper his meaningless reassurances in my ear. I lay there, feeling his unwanted caress, wishing like hell I was back in that pretty cage with the golden bars.

I felt his length plunging in and out of me, hearing his every little groan. He told me I was beautiful, and suddenly, I had never felt uglier.

When the first tear slipped free, my soul cracked. When my body began reacting to what he was doing, it cracked a bit more.

Breathin became a struggle. I was giving another part of me away to someone who would never in a thousand different lifetimes deserve it.

When he touched his lips on mine, my eyes flew open.

"No," I choked out.

"Don't be like that." He tried again, and this time, I turned my face.

His responding laugh was like nails on a chalkboard assaulting my eardrums.

I thought what happened next would be as bad as it could get—when he slid his hand down between us and began touchin a part of me not even Noah bothered with.

"Stop," I demanded, shoving at his arm. He ignored me, pinning a forearm across my chest and picking up his pace.

"Feels good, don't it?" he taunted, thrusting harder.

I ignored that.

My body thought it did; my mind though it was the worst form of torture I could go through. I focused on his right bicep, where the same V tattoo the other man had was inked. I'd come many times from my own fingers to know what was happening inside me.

There was the familiar tightening in my lower stomach, the pressure slowly building.

I willed it away, thinking every demented thought I could. I dragged the memory of Cali drilling into a man's dick to the forefront of my mind.

I thought of the precise way the cannibals had used a crowbar to break my uncle's ribcage apart right in front of me.

The distraction worked. It didn't take Vitus long to finish; I held onto those minutes like a lifeline. When he finally buried himself one last time, coming with a vomit-inducing moan, I forced his cock out of me before it had stopped twitching.

He hopped up with a smile I wanted to punch off.

"Damn, look at this." He grabbed his softening dick and thumbed off some of my body's obvious betrayal. Without warning he reached out and wiped it down the side of my face, laughing when I knocked his hand away.

I pulled my dirty slip back down and diverted my gaze to my toes as he tucked himself away.

"Well, I can't say you're the best I've ever had. I'm not really into corpses, but the others might be."

I jack-knifed into a standing position so fast, he took a cautionary step away from me. "What do you mean the others?"

As he pulled his shirt back over his head and let it fall into place, I already knew the answer. Why did I think it would end with him? I was an idiot.

Without giving any indication I was about to bolt, I darted towards the bathroom, paying no mind to the semen slowly sliding down my inner thigh.

There was a flimsy lock on the door. I knew in the recess of my mind that the move was illogical and did nothing but buy me maybe a few minutes. I went for it anyway.

He didn't try to stop me. I made it inside, slammed the door, and slid the deadbolt into place.

A creak sounded, followed by footsteps, and I knew his family had filed back into the room.

"Where the fuck she go?"

"She locked herself away. I didn't have to force her. She willingly let me between them legs. I told her one of you was next. I don't think she likes ya'll as much as she did me," Vitus joked.

He made me sound like a whore. I sort of felt like one too. In my head, I hadn't willingly given him a damn thing. But that wasn't true, was it?

"Get her outta there," the man named Vance ordered. I assumed that directive was given to Noah.

"Petals?" his soft voice called out to me not a minute later.

My heart crashed against its cavity. I'd been terrified plenty of times, but never like this. My eyes darted all around the room, stopping on the toilet.

The whole pre-conceived notion I'd had of throwing a battle to win the war seemed so naively childish then.

I didn't have a chance of winning anything, so why not go down swinging?

"Petals, open the door," Noah tried again.

"My name isn't fuckin Petals!" I lifted the top piece off the water tank and curled my fingers around the rim. Scampering backward, I made my way to the furthest corner and slid down the wall.

I brought my knees to my chest and watched the door. Adrenaline had my clenched hands shaking around the chunk of porcelain. Too many voices began murmuring at once for me to understand what it was they were saying.

They ceased abruptly. A millisecond later, the lock hit the dull tiled floor, and the weak wooden door blasted into the wall. I rose to my feet as Hawke barreled into the room.

He came straight for me, taking notice of the toilet lid a breath too late. I swung with everything I had, connecting with his dome.

"Sonofabitch!" He clutched the side of his head and stumbled sideways.

Vance was right behind him, and I wasn't lucky a second time. I swung at him with a heaving growl spilling from my lungs. He dodged it, grabbing hold of the lid and easily pulling it from my hands after a four-second struggle.

I wasn't expecting him to return the favor. When the lid hit the side of my forehead, pain had my mind going blank long enough for him to grab me by the legs and drag my shock-slackened body almost clear out of the bathroom the second I hit the floor.

Noah was yelling now, and someone else was yelling right back. Whatever they were saying was of no interest to me.

I somehow managed to grab hold of the door frame in a pathetic attempt to get away from Vance.

"Let go!" I struggled to break free by kicking him as best I could.

"You little bitch," a recovered Hawk spat down at me, slamming his booted heel right where four of my fingers were resting, making me let go of the doorframe.

Pain seemed to be radiating from everywhere. Something wet was running down the side of my face, and I could feel throbbing in my left hand. I felt like a rose being trampled on the ground. Vance carelessly dragged me the rest of the way into the bedroom.

I was lifted up by my middle and dropped face-first back onto the bed, kept there by Vance pressing my face into the mattress.

I tried my best, tried with my whole heart and every ounce of fight I had within me to stop them from destroying who I was.

In the end, that's exactly what they did. Each of them participated. Vance went first, forcing his cock inside me just like his son had less than twenty minutes ago.

He was much rougher. The grip he had on my hair seemed to tighten with his every thrust, setting my scalp aflame.

I wish I could say I made it hard for him to enjoy himself, but truthfully, I wasn't any kind of match for him—or his family.

I thought it couldn't get worse, but I was wrong. Vance lifted me by the throat like I was nothin but a dirty dishrag. He lined himself up with my virgin ass as Rex took the front. They entered me after some sick countdown, both brutally unforgiving. The skin around the rim of my ass shredded, and blood leaked between my cheeks.

I felt as if a pole of flaming iron was searing me in two. I screamed and begged for them to stop, suffocating on my sobs.

My body wanted to turn in on itself but, even there, it hurt too badly.

I couldn't tell how long they passed me around like a chip bowl at a party, each of them taking however much they wanted.

In the end, it was Noah who gave me the water that led me to pass out.

He probably thought he was giving me some form of peace, but his help came after a round too many.

Everything changed for me that night. The cracks in my soul became too wide. There was nothing left to hold onto.

Chapter Four

Grimm

I tossed the last body into the pit, and signaled for it to be lit up.

One of the acolytes shuffled forward and dumped kerosene up and down the deep, lengthy ditch. Another followed, casually dropping matches, keeping his black hooded robe clear of the flames that instantly erupted.

The man I'd just tossed in blinked up at me, his eyes wide. He tried to lift his head off the broken legs he'd partially landed on, but didn't have the strength.

He couldn't do anything but let the fire slowly eat him alive, thanks to Cobra crushing his vocal cords.

Leaving the acolytes to it, I made my way back inside the house, stomping my boots on the welcome mat my sister had demanded be put down. The last thing I wanted to hear was Cali's mouth because I tracked dirt across her immaculate hardwood.

The open floor plan gave me a clear view of Romero standing in the kitchen. I glanced at the contents of the blender he was emptying into a glass as I made my way to the sink. "Milkshake?" I guessed, turning the faucet on with my elbow.

"Always fucking milkshakes. Oh, let me correct myself—always *vanilla* fucking milkshakes."

I smirked to myself in amusement. Ever since Bryson, Cali's personal guard, left to help guard Luca's skin farm, Romero was on full-time Cali duty.

"She's like a fucking bear. All she does is sleep, eat, and chafe my dick—in that order.

"And I'm not complaining about the first or last one, but she's been talking to me like she's lost her motherfucking mind."

I shook my head. "Could have gone my whole life without hearing that bit about your dick. It's just hormones."

"Well, fuck hormones," he retorted before wordlessly passing me the dirty blender on his way to the fridge.

I rinsed it out and loaded it into the dishwasher. When I was finished, I leaned against the granite countertop and continued watching him.

"And what is that supposed to be?"

He ignored me at first, like he always tended to do. When I continued to stare, he sat down the foil packet with little chocolate chunks in it and stared back at me with eyes so fucking dark it almost looked like he didn't have any.

"This is a glass. Inside this glass is a vanilla goat milk shake.

"On top of *that* is puffy white shit, and on top of *that* is expensive ass chocolate. Any other questions Grimm?"

"Nope," I grinned. Fucking with him was one of the many highlights of my day—second after killing a few motherfuckers. "Just wondering if my baby sister still had your balls in the palm of her hand."

"You know, now that you mention it, I'll be balls deep inside your baby sister's sweet, perfect fucking pussy here—as soon as she's done with this drink." He lifted the glass up and a smug ass grin took over his face, matching the one now wiped clean off mine.

"You leaving soon?" he asked, changing the subject as he went over to a cabinet.

"Uh huh."

"Come tell Cali bye, and I'll walk you out," he more demanded of me than told me, grabbing a straw before making his way out of the kitchen.

That's how it worked, and I had no issues with it. I willingly and loyally did the devil's bidding. I was one of his few confidants.

It was the devil I found a brother in, who gave me a purpose, a home, and a family.

I stood in the kitchen a few seconds longer, prepping to say goodbye to the sister I felt I'd just gotten back. I didn't do feely emotional, and she'd turned into a hormonal typhoon as of late. She'd always been a bit manically childish—not her fault—but shit was at a def-con level so getting outta here for a few days sounded like a mini vacation.

Even though we weren't that close in the beginning, I couldn't see life without her crazy ass. She fit right in with our eighty degrees of fucked upness. She made my closest friend slightly human again.

It was something I'd been wondering if I'd royally fucked up for myself, by failing the only woman who'd made a lasting impression on me in every way that mattered.

"Damn, Grimmy, you set yourself up for that one," Cobra laughed, interrupting my self-reflecting, waltzing around the corner with a little blonde who was damn near dragging her feet. By the fussed up strands of his red hair, it was obvious what they'd been doing.

"I take it from the lack of crocodile tears she isn't aware of what's coming next?"

"Oh, nah, I'm gonna her take to the play room. Thirsty." He shrugged and pulled out a water-bottle, shaking it at me to emphasize his point.

The blonde looked my direction for explanation, no doubt wondering what the play room was and why it would make her wish she'd never set foot in this house.

She wasn't going to get one—not from me. I didn't give a shit how badly he was going to torture her.

She'd put herself in this situation; they all did. It was all about being fucked by a Savage.

Now Romero was permanently out of the running, it left three potential candidates close enough to him to count as bragging rights for spreading their legs for someone at the top of our hierarchy.

They never took into account that they wouldn't live long enough to tell anyone. Shit had only gotten worse after it was known Cali had a ring on her finger.

Things were finally dying back down to normal now. Maybe they realized she was a little worse off in the head than we were. That took some fucking effort.

"Go get her settled, I'm heading out."

I left him with those parting words and made my way to the second level.

One of the large double doors leading into their bedroom was cracked. Knowing that was done for my benefit only, I walked in without knocking.

The shit I felt seeing my sister on Rome's lap as he cupped her round bump was foreign to me. Fuck, it was foreign for him.

I could admit I was happy—maybe even as far as excited—to have a niece or nephew sooner than later. Love and all the other bullshit didn't mean much to me, but I wasn't numb to everything.

Someone important was missing though, someone who should have been around for all this maternal motherly shit Cali was going through.

"It's D-day!" Her bold blue eyes met my brown ones and she beamed at me, sitting her half-empty glass on the nightstand, right by the pexi-glass casing that held the head of Romero's piece of shit of a father, David. There was a giant book of baby names resting on top of it.

"I'm about to take off."

"Well, where are your bags? Do you have food? Are you sure you—"

"I know where I'm going, and the sooner I leave, the sooner she'll be back." I wasn't going to mention who the fuck knew what shape Arlen was in. I didn't even want to think about it myself.

It took me twice as long as it should have to track her ass down to an exact location. The last bit of information wasn't something I would be sharing with my sister, whose childhood was full of the same type of bullshit. Me and Romero had agreed on that without argument.

I would let him know when I got to her, and he could handle the rest. I would be doing enough damage control when everything else we were keeping from her came to light.

She stood up and made her way towards me, looking as tiny as she always had, with exception of the bulge slightly lifting her black dress. Looking at the two of us, no one would ever suspect we were related. With the same dad, different moms, we were night and day.

She was white as snow—damn near an albino, her hair only a few shades darker. My hair was dark and my tan skin was covered in various tattoos, whereas she only had the inverted cross that marked her as a Savage.

I knew she was as much of a hugger as I was, so what her intention was for getting so close to me, I didn't know.

"You better be back soon then, or I'm coming to get you, and I don't care what the asshole behind me has to say about it."

"We both know your ass isn't going anywhere unless I fucking say so. You keep trying me and I'll tie you to the bed again," Romero cut in, coming up behind her.

She rolled her eyes, ignoring him. Then, she surprised me by grabbing my arm like a kid would their favorite teddy bear and squeezing it. Being I was a good few inches taller than her, I wound up looking down at the top of her head.

"I'll be back long before baby S is here," I said, knowing that would bring a smile to her face.

Romero took hold of her wrist and gently pulled her away from me. I stepped back, giving them privacy as he whispered something I more than likely didn't want to hear in her ear.

He kissed her, placed a light parting touch on her stomach, and then motioned for me to walk out, silently falling in step beside me when we were back in the hallway.

"Will you two kids be able to play nice while I'm gone?" I asked as we made our way out the front door.

"They got me here," Cobra butted in, pushing off the wall where he'd been waiting for us.

"I don't need relationship help from either of you dickheads."

We approached where my Fat Bob was sitting with saddlebags already secured on the rear end.

They stood back as I wrapped a black bandana around my mouth and nose, slipped on a pair of shades, and pulled my hood up. Normally, I didn't go to such an extreme, but the heat was bearing down and this was the best way to protect myself against the elements on the ride I had ahead of me.

Once my fingerless gloves were on, I slipped an atomic slug bag over my shoulders, making sure the handle of my ReaperTac was sticking out.

"We sticking to the same plan?" Cobra asked.

"Yeah, give me four days after tonight. Come through the parking garage."

He nodded and stepped forward to dap me. "Be safe, bro. I'll be seeing you soon. I got a reason to break the charger out now." His face lit up like a little kids and I shook my head.

"What?" I asked Romero when he crossed his arms and just looked at me.

"You know what," he replied flatly. "And you know I'm right."

I did know what he was saying, but I didn't have a response.

"She might hate me," I admitted out loud for the first time.

"Yeah, fucking right, she has no reason to hate you," Cobra scoffed, easily picking up on our roundabout conversation. "You're her stars and moon," he fluttered his lashes and stared at the sun.

I gave him a flat look.

Romero slightly shifted, pulling my attention back to him, and I knew whatever he was about to say had him feeling uncomfortable, which rarely happened.

"You know the only thing I want from Cali is her to never stop loving me? She's a psychotic bitch and pisses me off a good ten times a day, but she's everything to me.

"I don't think I'd be able to keep going if I lost her. Maybe I'm pussy for having that big a weakness, but I quickly learned not give a shit. I love that woman; she's my fucking queen. From the day she and that annoying as shit, loud mouth girl you got a soft spot for came rollin their asses down that hill and running through the woods, I knew she was it for me.

"You knew it too; I know you did. Don't deny yourself something like this. Trust me when I say she's the best thing that's ever happened to me, aside from that squishy alien in her stomach.

"You've always been a king in your own right; don't come back here without your queen. If you gag her ass in the process, you'd be doing me a favor."

I could count on one hand the number of times I'd been surprised. This took two fingers. Cobra had the same expression on his face as I did. That was the most emotional shit he'd said to either of us since we'd been kids.

Hugging him would probably get me dropped on my ass and be taking shit way too far, but I felt the love of a brother just as strong as I always had, if not stronger—for the blessing I didn't need but he gave me anyway, and the man he became for my sister.

"I agree with all the shit he just said," Cobra commented, grounding us back to our usual self-preserved demeanors as he usually did when shit got to an awkwardly silent level.

"Call me as soon as you settle with her," Romero said, back to normal programming.

He didn't like saying goodbyes because they were often final. We three lived up to every fucked up expectation people had of us, but what no one knew was that when we cared about someone, we cared with the all parts of us that could still give a shit.

I was loyal only to my family; it was because of that I vowed to track down someone that had been stolen from us. And I had. And Rome was right.

I climbed on my Fat Boy, gave a slight nod of my head, and turned the engine over.

Now, it was time to bring her home where she belonged.

Chapter Four

Arlen

I'd had enough.

I could no longer feel the steady rhythm of my heart. I felt cold and damned. There were these constant moments where I would disconnect. I was either numb or feeling everything at once.

I needed someone to shove me over the fuckin edge, or put me out of my misery. I was sinking; something murky was rising. My sky was falling, and the tides were turning.

I didn't know how much time had passed since Noah gave me to those men wrapped up in a pretty bow.

My body still hurt, but whether it was all in my head or physical, I couldn't process.

I think it was two or three days ago he'd come in and announced we would be moving again soon. His voice sparsely registered—I wish he'd shut up and save his breath, choke on his own words. I couldn't bring myself to pretend I cared about anything he had to say. He needed to find a hobby and spare me one single second more of his company.

I'd been having beautifully morbid daydreams lately. Every time I heard him speak, and every time I flashed back to the men who took what didn't fuckin belong to them, I drifted off into a catatonic place.

I envisioned their ligaments scattered in pieces, their entrails greedily devoured by the crows cawing outside my window as a I sang the counting song.

One for sorrow, two for mirth…

Those black carrion birds had become a source of comfort.

I imagined them arriving just to keep me company, as if they knew in their majestic little heads that this kind of loneliness was new to me.

See, I'd always been kind of a loner, but never intentionally. I laughed a bit too loud, and my soul was a tad too wild for me to ever really blend in with normal folks.

This was different, though. This kind of lonely came from feeling like I no longer knew myself. I'd known exactly who I was before, but I didn't know who I was becoming now.

I'd had typical vengeful notions just weeks ago. These twisted thoughts were foreign to me. I swear I'd lost my mind; it felt like I was slowly going insane.

My life had been completely shaken up and rearranged. I knew I would always be partially to blame for that, and that there was nothin to be done about the events that led me here.

I wasn't going to deny those facts.

I'd fucked up, but I was sick of thinking about all that was. I was tired of feeling lost.

I stood in the dull bathroom under a lackluster light and boldly dared to look at my reflection. Someone who didn't know what I'd been through would look at me and not see anything wrong, or anyone other than the same old Arlen Prosner.

The bruises between my thighs and missing patches of skin I'd scrubbed at too hard were only evident to me and the men who left them there. I couldn't shake the feeling of their heavy breath on my neck, or the way they felt me up.

No matter how many times I washed myself, I felt like I was coated in layers of grime and filth. My body was a temple, and they'd tainted it. Invisible scars weighed me down heavily.

Like a moth to a flame, my wings had burned away. I dug down deep inside myself, searching for the part of me that cared, but whatever it was that shifted had me caring a little less lately.

I wasn't sure about this new me. I thought I'd picked up all the broken pieces, but the ones I had didn't align anymore. This Arlen was a stranger, and she offered no explanation.

I'd waited for my shadow, but he never came. Turns out this whole surviving thing was pretty goddamn hard. It was even harder when you had nothing left to lose and all you felt was a cruel, never-ending wanting.

At what point did I stop facing denial and ask myself what I was struggling to survive for?

Chapter Five

Grimm

I rode for a full day and night to get where I needed to be, stopping only to refuel, knowing exactly the range my Fat Boy could handle before it would start to sputter.

On my final stop, I stashed the bike in the exact spot I'd mapped out the week prior, pre-fueling with the gas can I'd stashed under a caved in portion of the abandoned garage.

All that was left to do was wait.

I munched on smoked jerky and sipped some hooch to pass a little more time, before taking a piss and then prepping to move into a proactive position.

I snagged my ReaperTac from my bag, now secured with the others, and then attached the suppressor to my Glock 17 after checking the magazine. The black gun was simple to use, durable, ubiquitous, and took the most easy to obtain ammunition there was: 9 mm Parabellum.

Cutting through a few weed-covered yards, I moved closer to the house I knew Arlen was being held at. The heat was a sonofabitch, but the oncoming shadows helped to shade me from full on exposure.

I'd lived in this fucking place my entire life, spent half that time on the road, and still abhorred the sun. I couldn't stand its intensity or its light. I was a creature of the night.

The dark was easier on the eyes, and much better for killing, hunting, and getting pussy.

And that was why I'd planned to make my move when the sky was a deep purple and the

Badlands' natural terrain was only lit up by a crescent moon.

The house had been easy to find; it was the only dingy blue one in the entire run-down neighborhood. There was a dark green pickup truck parked right on the front lawn, and I watched a laughing Noah climb into it with three other men.

I wasn't there for him. Not this time. His hourglass was near empty enough. I couldn't wait to shred him apart with my bare hands. My objective right then was to get to my girl.

Not knowing how long they would be gone, I tracked the movement inside the house, trying to get a feel of the precise layout.

I needed to get Arlen out ASAP, but I was never one for rushing into shit without taking in as much detail as I could. Acting brashly got people killed for being complete dumbasses and not using their heads.

Me and my brothers learned that at fourteen when we sat back and watched a group of cannibals get slaughtered trying to steal a dairy cow, of all things.

The family had set traps around their property to prevent that very thing from happening. Lucky it was those fuckers and not us, because that's exactly what we'd been there to do.

We still ended up with the cow in the end; we just took out the family later that same day as they cleaned the bodies up. But it was still a beneficial learning lesson.

Carrion birds perched on the house's depleted rafters, and the dying tree off to the side of it. They had a habit of showing up when shit was about to go down around me.

I hadn't figured out why, and I couldn't lie and say it wasn't creepy the first few times this happened.

But as with everything else that shaped who I was, I'd come to like them, and it heavily attributed to my alias.

Estimating there were four people inside and that my girl was naturally being kept in the room with the plywood over the window like a caged animal, I moved.

Sticking to the darkest part of the shadows wasn't something I did intentionally. The dark had a way of gravitating towards me. I used it to cover me as I made my way to the side door and found my initial assumption correct: the dumb fucks inside hadn't locked it.

Easing the poor excuse of a barrier open, I slipped inside and reclosed it. Laughter sounded from the right…the living room. A pipe groaned as someone shifted closer in a room to my immediate left—a bathroom, I guessed.

Straight ahead of me were half missing stairs that led down to what had to be the basement.

Ascending the short three stairs off to the side of me that led to a small landing, I pushed another door open when I knew it was clear.

I stepped into a small hall that expanded outward into a filthy kitchen. There was a laundry room with a rusted washer and dryer caddy in the corner from where I stood, and another door was wide open across from it.

By the low grunt and pair of jeans I could see around a set of hairy ankles, someone was taking a shit in a toilet that didn't work. There was a distinct stench emanating through the hall that could only have come from other people having done the same thing before him, and leaving all the feces to build up.

I readied my Glock and eased towards the bathroom. The suppressor wasn't going to completely silence the shot—this wasn't an action film—but it would reduce the muzzle flash and confuse the others in the house as to what they'd heard or where it had come from.

The man had his head buried in his hands when I pulled the trigger.

I'd just done him a favor. The kill was fast, instead of fatally wounding.

He didn't have time to react, and even if he did, it wouldn't have mattered much.

The bullet burned flesh as it formed a circular hole rimmed with abraded skin right in the top of his dome. It slid right through his hair and muscle, as if it were a silken caress. The casing made quick shrapnel of his calcium, phosphorus, sodium, and collagen case before splitting apart tissue and fibrous membranes.

All that gorgeous handiwork from a little bullet, and he was gone in a fraction of a second, without getting a moment to admire it or feel the inside of his head being ripped apart. The only thing he left behind was the smell of shit and a spray of blood, bone, and brains on the wall.

Hearing what sounded more like a loud door slamming than a gunshot, the other people in the house immediately began to investigate.

I slipped across the hall to the laundry room and waited, placing the Glock in my waist band in place of my ReaperTac.

There was a loud “What the hell?”, before one of them opened the front door, another took the stairs to the second floor, and the third came my direction, calling out the name of his dead friend.

Not getting a response, he peered into the bathroom, recoiling like a spring the second he saw the body slumped at an odd angle.

Before he could react, I moved from my position. He never saw me coming. I clamped a hand over his mouth and nose to shut him the fuck up and muffle the expulsion of air I knew would be coming.

Instead of slicing into his neck, I stabbed my curved stainless steel blade into the side, going through an artery, and gripped the handle a little tighter, dragging downward.

Most of his blood ran down his throat instead of spilling out all over the damn floor. His body lowered with silent spasms. He tried to speak, asphyxiating on his own ichor.

This was always messy, and I tried not to make it too gory.

The method of the kill wasn't what excited me. Neither did the begging or the torture—not that I didn't enjoy those aspects of my work. It was the final outcome, death, that made all this worth it.

The moment when someone realized their life was slipping away was my favorite part of the job. No matter what they did or how they lived, death would always show up in the end. I merely helped conduct their souls to the afterlife.

I liked my job. I was *good* at my job—so fucking good even the devil admired my craft. I had to live in hell, so why not enjoy myself and purge some motherfuckers from it?

I left the man behind and made my way through the rest of the house. Whoever had gone out the front door was nowhere to be seen. He could wait.

Darting towards the stairs, I swapped melees again and popped the man who'd started coming back down as I was going up, sending a slug right between his eyes.

I sidestepped as his body took a tumble past me, landing at an obtuse angle below and leaking blood onto the floor.

At the top step, I saw there was only one closed door out of three. I didn't even bother trying to undo the excessive number of locks on the outside. I kicked the piece of shit right in.

And there she was.

She was sitting in a barely lit room on a full sized bed with rope wrapped around her wrists. There was an almost crushing feeling of relief that coursed through my chest merely from seeing her again. I felt like I'd just found something I didn't know I'd lost.

Her reaction was delayed. I knew then that she was different.

I wasn't surprised by that—nor did we have time to sing a sad song about it, but damn did it fuck with my chest a little bit.

She studied me as if she wasn't sure I was real. I did my damndest to make sure my eyes didn't stray from her face. Whatever the fuck she had on left little to the imagination.

I focused on her eyes that reminded me too much of sunlight and spoke a vocabulary that was all their own. I didn't dwell on the fact that I understood the language because it was mine. I didn't dwell on what the darkest part of my subconscious mind already knew. That whatever just fucking happened between us when I kicked in the door was the magnifying of a spark that would soon be an inferno.

Instead, I told her to get the fuck up and that we needed to go.

Chapter Six

Arlen

I was leaving the bathroom as he was entering the bedroom.

He had what looked twine partially bunched up in his hands, and one of his cronies standing in the hall behind him.

My face gave away exactly what I was thinkin: wrapping that damn rope around his neck and cutting off every ounce of oxygen flowing to his brain.

I could watch him gasp for air, and when he thought it was over, I'd give him breath just so I could swiftly take it away again.

I spotted the prod in this new man's hand. I was the first to speak, surprising both of us, "He supposed to be your protection?" My voice sounded so hollow I tried to pinpoint when the last time I'd used it was.

"After this morning's incident, I thought it would be best."

Course he did. It was all fun and games until I was launching bowls of steaming oatmeal at his face. But I thought that had happened days ago.

"I need to leave, and timing is kind of urgent, so if you could just…" He twirled his finger in the air, signaling for me to turn around.

I wasn't willingly giving him my back. Crossing my arms tightly over my chest, I slightly widened my stance, as if I were a bull preparing to charge. "Why is it urgent?"

"I don't have time for this. Turn around, or I'll have him give you a zap."

He took a step closer, instantly retracing it when I did the same.

Why had I never realized he was afraid of me? Vitus had done the same thing. I was just a girl, after all. I wondered where he was goin that had a light sheen of perspiration on his sullen skin. How much had I missed happening around me?

I silently held my wrists out in front of me and gave him a blank stare. If I was gonna be tied up, I preferred my arms to be in front of me. With no further demands, he quickly secured the rope, pulling so tightly I let out a small grunt as the brittle rope dug into my skin.

"I'll unbind you when I return. This is just a precaution."

I could've pointed out that I was locked behind a door in a house full of men…there wasn't much to be cautious of on my end, but I had nothing to say to him.

He turned and wordlessly left me alone with what almost looked like concern on his face.

I took my usual position back up, studying the rope to see if I could possibly escape.

I was still doing that when the first pop spilled through the ventilation system. Unlike the last time, I knew it wasn't a rat. Voices from below and rapid footfalls made me think it was just men rough-housing.

Someone came up the stairs, but didn't come into the room, and then I heard it again. It was much closer this time around, and followed by something—some*one*—falling down the steps.

When the door flew open, I didn't even jump. Staring at the massive hooded figure, I thought I'd either officially lost my mind or that I wasn't awake. He shifted only slightly, making himself appear even taller, and looked me straight in the eye.

I knew those eyes. I saw the beard. Saw the inverted cross I'd always wanted to touch.

I even remembered the scent of citrus sweet and spicy wood that was naturally his. The hairs rose on the back of my neck as we simply stared at one another.

I couldn't tell ya what it was that happened right then, only that I suddenly felt more awake then I had in days. Yet I still wasn't fathoming what was going on. Leave it to Grimm to open his mouth and give me some swift clarification while skipping over all casualties.

"Get the fuck up; we need to go." He glided towards me like he was floating on air, and pulled what looked like a mini scythe from beneath his black ensemble. The blade on the damn thing had to be a good seven inches long. And was that blood?

I instinctively brought my arms up, but it was more in defense than for him to slice through the rope like he did. It fell away, landing on the floor as if it were a dead snake.

It didn't truly register that his hand was wrapped around mine and he was pulling me out into the hall until I realized my legs were moving. He didn't launch into detail about what would happen next, but he wasn't a real talkative man in the first place. That clearly hadn't changed.

The striped wallpaper in the hall hung in peeled sheets, revealing moldy grey walls underneath. It sounded like the warped wood flooring was going to cave in from the pressure of our weight, sending us straight to the basement I knew the rats dwelled in. I'd been able to hear them in the vents when the house was quiet.

We were halfway down the stairs when I saw the body at the bottom. I couldn't bring myself to feel sorry for him. I didn't even try.

With no shoes on my feet, I made sure to avoid the crimson puddle just like Grimm did.

At the sound of footsteps, Grimm brought me flush against his back and pulled out a shiny black gun.

I didn't see the initial impact the bullet made with the man's face, but his screech of pain was somethin similar to the sound a cat made if you stepped on its tail.

When we started moving again, I saw him holding a hand over the spot his right eye should have been, blood rushing through the gaps in his fingers in a waterfall effect. He fell backward into the wall, making that same high-pitched sound.

I didn't feel sorry for him either. He deserved this serving of vigilante justice.

My nerves felt like live-wires ready to short circuit, like at any moment I would wake up. This would have all just been a corporal daydream from me being stuck in my head again. I barely noticed how hard I was squeezing Grimm's hand, and when I did, I found myself squeezin it harder.

He couldn't let me go. He had to take me with him.

I didn't care what his rep was; he was a much better alternative than being left behind with any of these men.

The first floor of the house was in the same condition as the second, if not worse. I didn't understand why Noah was even staying someplace like this. He was used to more luxuries than I had been; a true spoiled pig.

We went through a kitchen and entered a hall with a strong noxious odor I couldn't place. Bypassing two doorways, I saw a dead man on a toilet, and another with his throat split open. I would be a liar if I said I wasn't impressed with how fast Grimm got this all done.

He took me down two stairs and right out a side door. Darkness was waiting for us, as were the few carrion birds I'd made friends with.

Grimm looked back at me and, without warning, turned and scooped me up as if I were a ragdoll before proceeding to take off.

"What are you doin?" I asked, holding onto him as he nearly ran with me in his arms.

"No shoes," he answered, seeming to know exactly where he was going.

It didn't take all that long for us to reach a garage, leaning on its last leg. He sat me down and immediately went inside, still givin me zero explanation as to what was goin on.

When he came back out, it was from around the corner of the structure, and he was wheeling a blacked out customized bike. I only knew it was a Harley because it said so right on a black front panel. The tires were thick, and the pipes gleamed; had this been a different situation, I might've drooled over the damn thing. It was so fitting for Grimm to have such a thing.

"Put this on," he gruffly demanded, thrusting the large black hoodie he'd had on just a second ago into my line of vision.

I took a quick glance at him and saw he was focusing real hard on everything that wasn't beneath my neckline.

That filthy feeling I always had intensified.

He was probably well aware of what had happened in that room. Did it make him think worse of me? Unable to look at him a second longer, I snatched the garment and pulled it over my head. It was long, covering everything, and almost to my knees. And it had his familiar smell. I left my hair tucked down inside it and pulled up the hood, knowing I was gonna have to get on his bike.

"Come on," he said, swinging a leg over the side. I moved so I was behind him and tried to copy his flawlessly executed move with no help, but wound up gripping his shoulder.

"Easy," he warned.

Trying again, I lifted up my slip and his hoodie and was able to take root behind him on my next attempt.

"Hold on tight," he said over his shoulder, turning the engine over. I did as I was told and wrapped my arms around his middle, smashin my breasts into his back and clinging to him as he hit the gas and propelled us into the road.

Two kids and what looked like their grandmother stood in their front yard three houses down.

A bug zapper was lit up and illuminated what they was doing. They stopped mid-dig of whomever the person was they were burying to watch us pass. A tiny wooden cross stuck lop-sided out of the ground with the word MOM written on it in tiny red letters.

As Grimm sharply turned the corner, the older child lifted her chubby hand and waved at me, smiling in spite of death being right in front of her.

At her age, seeing something like that in my neighborhood would have been hard for me to wrap my head around. It would have never happened in Centriole in the first place.

For this young girl, it was just another day in the Badlands. A child understood reality much better than I'd ever had the chance to at such a young age.

Like many of the other folk out here she had a family and she was educated. She had to wake up every day and go to sleep like everybody else did. Only, unlike the people livin nice and comfortably in The Kingdom, she wasn't guaranteed to survive and see another day.

She understood what this world was really like, and still found it in her heart to smile. In my mind, she was already stronger than I ever was. And as I was taken away from that old neighborhood, I came to realize somethin.

That wall didn't protect a damn thing. It just crippled everyone behind it.

Chapter Seven

Arlen

When we hit the open road, he gunned us forward, roaring full speed ahead.

I waited for Noah to come crashing into my whimsical bubble and drag me back to the real world where my wrists were bound and I was alone on that bed, waitin for him to have his way with me again, but he never came.

It was just me and Grimm. Of all the people I thought would come and get me, I always knew it'd be him. He had always been my shadow.

Just when I was ready to give it all up, he came kickin doors in and remindin me he'd never let that happen. I held onto his waist a little tighter, but felt no fear in this moment.

The starless sky was like a black swirling sea overhead. It was the first beautiful thing I'd seen in months. The vast wasteland looked picturesque like this. Wind whipped at my face and made my eyes burn, but I didn't care. It was fresh and clean, filtering in and out of my corrupted lungs—another sign that I'd really been freed from my four-walled prison.

The faster Grimm went, the more I felt the little tick in my chest that had been long gone trying to sputter again.

There was a chill in the air, but his hoodie gave me comfort, and his solid body was like a mini heater. He was the realest thing of all, the final bit of proof that this was reality. I could feel his firm abdominal muscles beneath my palms and smell him with every breath I took.

I'm not sure how long we rode, but when he finally began to slow, my arms ached and my thighs burned. There were structures rising up in the near distance and I belatedly realized I was looking at a city.

He pulled off to the side of the road and cut the engine. "You need to piss?" he asked, easily swinging off the bike and turning to face me.

For real? His face was so serious I had the absurd urge to laugh—and that was really somethin I was certain I'd forgotten how to do. How long had I been with him? An hour? Three? I could almost imagine that awful shithole of a house was months behind me already.

But my barren feet had felt the wind just as clearly as my cheeks. The slip I had on was still covered by nothing other than his hoodie, and I still felt filthy. It was impossible to look at him for longer than a few seconds, and I'd never had that problem before.

His gaze was penetratin. I forgot how easily he could see right through me.

Then there was the whole other issue that I couldn't even believe was happening at a time such as this. The way this man pulled me in over and over again, like gravity I couldn't overcome. I tried damn hard, too. I had been since the day we met. He would be a bad habit I'd never break free of.

I was in no kind of state to indulge in him. My mind was too unstable, brimming with an ugly cyclone of hatred, pain, and rage.

My soul had divided in two, and somethin wicked had taken residence in the middle. I didn't want him looking at this version of Arlen Prosner, but I wasn't much of a fan of the old one, either.

All of that sobered me right up and killed my momentary joy. I was like a mockingbird that could no longer carry a tune. And what was a mockingbird without its song, now that its whole purpose was gone?

The strange part of me I wasn't real acquainted with yet had an answer, but she still withheld it. Grimm stood before me, strong as ever, like he was the one who would explain everything, as if it was his responsibility to shoulder my burdens and make it better.

And wasn't that bullshit? Hadn't I handled everything up until this point? A harsh resounding *no* swiftly echoed inside my head. I didn't understand that either, so I wasn't goin to bother trying.

Clearing my throat, I shook my head, putting on the best poker face I could. Not a second later, his hand was cuppin my chin and reorienting my face with his line of vision.

"When I speak to you with words, you give me your eyes and speak back. That's how a conversation works."

"Plenty a people talk without payin attention to what the other's doin, Grimm."

I scowled and pushed his hand away; he easily let me go, but then snapped his fingers in my face to make me focus on him again.

“Last I checked, we’re not plenty of people. I want your eyes on mine. You got that, brat?”

It sounded like he’d left somethin hangin off his sentence, but I knew Grimm well enough that if he didn’t elaborate the first time, he wouldn’t be goin back to amend his words.

Besides, he’d just called me brat. I didn’t think I’d ever hear that nickname again. To be honest, I’d hated it, but ya know somethin? Brat sounded a helluva lot better than Arlen at the moment.

“I don’t have to go number one or number two,” I answered, holdin his gaze a full seven seconds—I counted.

“That’s an improvement, but you could’ve just said you don’t have to take a shit.”

“I don’t talk like you, Grimm.”

“Clearly,” he grunted, going to the saddlebag on the opposite side of his bike.

“You shouldn’t have an issue looking people in the eye. Why would you want to hide that face of yours?”

I blinked. Was that sarcasm? If he’d just complimented me, I might still be daydreamin. When I just stared at him like an illiterate fool, he opened the bag and pulled out a pile of clothing.

He wordlessly held the bundle in his hands, waiting for me to get off his Harley and put it on right there on the side of the road. I climbed down, feeling like I’d just stepped in a bowl of Jell-O.

“Careful,” he warned, shooting a hand out to steady me by grabbing my shoulder.

“I’m good,” I said after a few seconds, taking the small pile from him. I sorted everything out, surprised to find a pair of underwear and a bra folded inside the dark green tank top.

Seeing as we were on the shoulder and out in the open, I dressed as quick as I could.

I slipped the black underwear on, then the fitted charcoal pants. Next were the brown leather combat boots. A pair of socks had been shoved down inside them. I reckoned Cali was to thank for all the extras—the girl had smarts.

Once the shoes were laced, I pulled Grimm's hoodie over my head and turned around, giving him my back as I took off the slip and clasped the matching bandeau bra.

Little bumps peppered my skin as it was exposed to the night air. Snagging the tank top, I hurriedly added that last, and tried to ignore the feel of Grimm's eyes on me the entire time.

"What now?" I asked, turning to face him the second I was decent.

"I have to go into the city—"

"You ain't leavin me," I butted in.

"Never planned on leaving you, brat, I just thought you'd like to be dressed before we went."

That was logical. “Oh, well, here.”

“Keep it.” He ignored his outstretched hoodie and climbed back on his bike.

Shruggin my shoulders, I pulled it back over my head, pushing the sleeves up as best I could, and then climbed back on behind him, trying not to pay much attention to how sore my ass had become.

This was nothin compared to what it’d felt like…whenever that incident was. He gunned his engine again and we were off, leaving my slip of ruined material behind us.

Chapter Eight

Grimm

She didn't need to hold me so tight, but I wasn't going to stop her.

This was the only time I'd had a woman sitting on the back of my bike instead of dragging them behind it. Being held like this was different, but not as intolerable as I'd imagined.

I tried not to think about it too much, how right it felt. I focused on wondering why I'd said what I had. I'd been trying to tell her she had too pretty a face to hide it away.

That was an understatement, anyway. Brat was a bombshell. It knocked me off kilter to even think that. I had almost eleven years on her, but my moral compass hadn't spontaneously decided to start working again because of that.

This thought process was more along the lines that I'd been with women all over the spectrum—beautifully dark to pale, freckled redheads, and none of them looked like her. They weren't even a fraction as enticing; they'd still be alive if that were the case.

I could only imagine how much better she'd look at this age. I could see it clear enough that my dick hardened as we tore up the blacktop, and I was in no position to fix it.

That was a good enough reason to concentrate on other matters, like getting inside her head on our trip home.

Not sounding like a pubescent little boy was a good start. That bullshit that just came out of my mouth was cringe-worthy.

Not only was it a corny ass line, but it didn't exactly translate what I'd been thinking clearly. Speaking to women wasn't in my repertoire of skills. I was usually telling them to shut the fuck up for screaming in my ear. That was in both instances: fucking and killing.

Cobra was the best at things like that; even Romero was smoother than I was, and he wasn't Casanova by anyone's standards—not even my sister's.

I could tell by the look on Brat's face that she didn't know if I'd been bullshitting or serious. That blank mask she always tried to slip on might as well have been invisible. She had always been easy for me to read, like a picture book—I didn't need to an utter a word, and neither did she.

I just got her.

I don't think she was aware of that until now. She hadn't been aware of a lot of things.

That was the problem with people from The Kingdom: they didn't live in reality.

They lived in a fantastical dreamland, and when reality showed up, they were fucked.

I wasn't blaming Brat for her lack of life experience, because neither of us could help where we came from. And though I was no better than the fuckers that had just had her—in fact, I knew I was worse in a few key categories—I refused to condone what I was fully aware had been done.

I wasn't going to coddle her, though, and I wasn't going to ask if she was okay. That was a dumbass rhetorical question. There were some things you just didn't need to confirm. Her eyes were open windows that gave it all away.

I understood the language they continued to speak, even if she didn't.

The fire that had once lit up her entire being like a beacon now burned within a darkness inside her that could rival my own.

She needed to be educated.

She needed to learn that there was nothing in the dark to be afraid of. I wasn't going to save her from it.

I wasn't a hero. I never would be—not for her.

We were all born to live in this hell. I would teach her how to transcend and thrive in it. I would drain her, break her down if I had to, just so I could be the one to make her whole again. In my mind, it *had* to be me.

I'd felt the need to shadow her from the beginning, and this situation only strengthened that resolve. I'd lost enough in this world. I wouldn't let it take her, too.

I would show her that hell could be beautiful. This is where she belonged—right beside me. Even knowing what my lifestyle meant for her…it was too late for that now.

Ask me where the fuck all this was coming from and I wouldn't have an exact answer.

I'd never had anything to be selfish about until her.

No one had ever looked at me like Brat did, seeing more than a man who harvested souls for a living…like I was something worth giving a fuck about.

Cali and my brothers tried to show me that very thing, but it wasn't the same. I knew Romero would know how to explain it better than I could. Logic, reason, rationality…none of it mattered. I just had this uncontrollable urge to protect her. I'd failed before—completely.

Had I been paying attention to her like I'd always done up until that night, she would have never made it out of the house. Had whatever this was between us been out in the open, no one would have dared remove her from that house. People were too afraid of me to ever fuck with someone who belonged to me.

I'd taken my eyes off her for what seemed like only a minute, and then she was gone.

That wouldn't happen again.

I would make her unequivocally mine. May some divine power have mercy on anyone who ever had the balls big enough to try and get between us again. I sure as fuck wouldn't.

Chapter Nine

Arlen

A faded green sign welcoming people to Rivermouth rose up on our right. It was marked with the Sigil of Baphomet, an inverted pentagram with the horned head of a goat. I knew the counterclockwise Hebrew characters spelled out Romero's name. He truly was the devil in the flesh. To think I'd once been terrified of meeting him or any of his satanic acolytes…They'd wound up being my closest friends, my extended family.

Life was most certainly a pretentious bitch, but she had her moments. I shifted on the seat so I could have a better view.

I'd heard every other city had been abandoned, which was hard for me to believe when I took into account that the population of Centriole didn't house *that* many damn people—not to mention the fact that I'd also heard that others were still managing to thrive. Not on a scale such as The Kingdom, but still: they were active.

Grimm didn't slow like I expected him to; if anything, he sped up the second he flicked his high beams off, whipping past moss covered buildings, a car left in the middle of the street, and avoiding a large pothole. How the hell could he see so well in the dark?

I squealed when he took a corner so fast I thought we were going to tip. I could've touched the asphalt if I'd wanted to—easily.

I felt him vibrate with laughter as I hid my face in his back, snuggling down in his long hoodie.

When I dared look back up, it was to see him coasting into the parking garage of a huge brick building with pointed arches.

He went up to deck C and swung the bike into a parking space in a darkened corner nearest a steel door.

Soon as the engine was cut, he was off the bike and gently lifting me down to the ground, supporting me until he was sure I was steady on my feet.

Moving with fluid vitality, he detached the largest bag from the back of his motorcycle and took my hand. I stuck close to him, looking all around the expansive space, expecting somethin to jump out at us at any second.

"Why are we here?" I asked in a low whisper.

"Didn't trust you to stay awake the full length of the ride, and I don't think you'd like falling off the back of the bike."

I wasn't tired.

When he pushed open the steel door, I was even more awake. Why did he pick this of all places to make a pit stop?

I wasn't sure if my curiosity was in full effect because I'd been stuck in the same environment day in and day out, or because I'd never seen anything like this.

The curved moon was the only thing trying to light our way, and there'd only been one window at the top of the stairwell.

Obviously the old elevator didn't work—not that I would trust it in the first place—so we walked. I held onto Grimm, hoping I didn't trip over somethin right in front of me, and because I wasn't touching the railing beside us.

He pushed open another door and we entered a super long hallway, lit only a little better.

That's when I realized we were in a gigantic hospital. It looked like somethin straight out of a horror film.

I was immediately more intrigued. The air was dusty, the paint on the walls so chipped they looked layered in mulch.

He continued down the hall with me in tow, maneuvering around an old wheelchair I would have run right into.

Our boots crunched over sheets of paper, grime, and some trash littering the floor. A few reinforced windows lined the wall on our left, but they were so dirty it was nearly impossible to see out of em.

I was going to ask why we were there again when he abruptly turned, just as we reached the end of the hall and entered a room. When he dropped my hand, I grabbed his shirt.

If he minded, he didn't voice it. He silently pushed the door shut and unzipped his bag.

A second later, a soft florescent glow lit up our surroundings. He'd pulled out what looked like a kiddy lantern.

"Have you been here already?" I asked, noticing how tidy the room was. I answered my own question when I saw the semi-clean patient bed with a fresh floral blanket on it.

"When I had a general idea of where you were, I began planning out a route there and back. This hospital was the best place. It's more than fifteen buildings, empty, as you can see, and ideal to hole up compared to the abandoned, roach-infested motel around the corner. I sent one of the acolytes out to make sure it was clear and set up a place you could sleep," he explained.

I think that was the most words he'd ever spoken to me in one go. His voice was deep, but also a little gravelly. I'd say very manly, but I hadn't ever been around any men of his caliber to make such a statement.

He turned to face me, and I was able to hold his gaze for a full four seconds before I pretended there was somethin else more intriguing to look at. Course there wasn't. He had always been the most interestin person in my life.

Well, outside of Cali, who was a whole other special story, and the reason I'd met him in the first place.

If that cannibal hadn't carried her crazy self into the barn that day, I wouldn't be alive. I was sure his rotting corpse was thinkin twice about that decision.

I wondered how she'd dealt with all that happened to her. She'd been used since she was just a little girl, and that made me sick to my stomach. Sure, she grew up to be a lil different, but she did grow—and change—and she was the strongest woman I knew. But she'd also fully embraced the crazy inside her. She wasn't as unsure of it as I was mine.

“Brat,” Grimm said, suddenly in front of me and pullin me outta my head. I had to tilt my chin to look at him.

“Don’t do that, either.” He said it simply enough, but there was an edge to it.

“You can’t tell me not to think.”

“I didn’t tell you not to think. I told you not to keep it in, and that you can talk to me.”

I was gonna point out that he most certainly hadn’t said any of that, but I wasn’t going to get lengthy dialogue from Grimm. I’d never needed it before. I just got him. Without really trying, it was like some natural phenomenon between us, just as the sun knew when to trade places with the moon.

Still, what the heck happened during our separation? Why did he now want me to confide in him? He was back to staring me down at this point, and I was close to having a emotional outburst from it, so I did the next best thing and hugged him.

I knew he wasn't any kind of hugger, but I didn't care. I smashed my face against his firm chest, purposely breathed him in, and tightly embraced him. I waited for him to shove me away, but he just stood there for a full minute. Then, he hugged me back.

I probably could have died right then from the sheer impact that had on my chest. His arms around me was the first thing that had felt right in a very long time.

He made me feel somethin other than numb.

"Thank you," I said, reluctantly pulling away. I dropped my arms but he kept his firmly on my back.

"Why are you thanking me?"

"You came for me."

He made a sound in the back of his throat and stepped away, turning back to his bag. I got the feelin I'd said the wrong thing. I didn't care. My mouth had gotten me this far; what was a bit of truth gonna do now?

Plus, we could both use some dosage of feelings in our lives.

"I know I was too late, and you might be wondering why I'm not treating you like a piece of glass, but that's not me, and I'm not going to do that."

"It's also not like you to be this open," I couldn't help but point out.

"Not being open was a mistake we're going to rectify. You only talk to me," he was quick to clarify.

"That sounds rather possessive of you."

"Should I warn you that I'm going to be selfish and protective over the only thing that's ever been exclusively mine?"

Yeah, I was probably still dreamin. I opened my mouth, or it was already hangin open in what was either shock or a confused state of cautionary joy—I wasn't sure. "Did you just call me a thing?" was my brilliant reply to what were potentially the best words I'd ever heard in my meager life.

He reached out and gently took hold of my hand, leading me to the bed. Without a word, he directed me to sit. I sank down on what felt like a plush piece of Styrofoam beneath the floral blanket, and focused on his chin.

He was onto me, and used his finger to aim my head up so we had eye connection before he said anything else. "You're *my* thing—pain in the ass, bratty hellion. Call me a possessive dick if it makes you feel better. Still my thing."

He went returned to his bag, giving me his back to scowl at. What was I supposed to say to any of that? Why the hell did he have to come out all noble now?

"First of all, Grimm, I'm a woman, not a thing. Second of all, if I'm anything of yours—"

"You're my woman, then. Is that better? And I'm your man. I had some advice given to me, and was reminded that this was inevitable. You and me both know it, so let's not do that bullshit."

"Label it however you need to. I'll leave the room if you want so you can do the girl thing and cry, maybe throw a tantrum and break whatever you can pick up, but it's not going to change anything."

I went back to scowling, but I wasn't upset with him. Granted, the man could have worded that much, much better. I wasn't expecting flowery poetry from him, though.

I wasn't expecting any of this. I knew in the back of my mind he was right about this being inevitable—in the fantasy land I lived in, where my feels weren't one-sided, that is.

I hadn't ever been certain he knew how I felt. It was never discussed. It was just a shared look here or there. He saw right down to the bare bones of my soul. I should've known better. Course he'd known.

"You hungry?" he asked, standing up again from his crouching position.

"So we're gonna just move right along then? That's it?"

"Are you hungry?"

"No, I'm not hungry, Grimm. Don't change the subject, either."

"Eat this." He threw something through the air.

As it came towards my face, I instinctively reached up and caught it. A damn red apple.

"I just said I wasn't hungry."

"You lied," he confidentially retorted, and at that very second my stomach snarled in agreement.

I bit into the apple so I didn't launch it as his smirking face. I wasn't goin to admit it was the juiciest apple I'd ever tasted. He came over with his own, and a plastic bottle, sitting down right beside me.

I didn't pay close attention to the way his tattoos I'd committed to memory looked in the light, or how perfectly sculpted his body was beneath his black shirt. I didn't even notice the little strand of hair that had fallen out of place and now sort of rested on his forehead.

We sat there munching in silence until he lifted the bottle up and took a swig. I watched his throat bob as he swallowed. He held out to me when he was done, and I slowly took it, staring down at the clear liquid inside.

I knew this wouldn't be laced—Grimm wouldn't do that—but it was a sure reminder of all the times I'd had some that had been.

It's just water, I told myself. Somethin I'd drank plenty of times before Noah came along. Damn. Noah. He was still out there.

"You don't want me like this." That was the simplest way I could say I was a mess without having to go into detail.

He looked at the ceiling for a few seconds. "I'm not good at this shit, Brat," he sighed, rolling his shoulders. "I want you whatever way I can have you. Any version of you is better than none at all, and this one is perfect for me."

See, I knew he'd understand what I was sayin without me having to elaborate. He didn't disappoint.

"Who told you you're not good at this, Romeo?" I teased with a smile.

"Romero is better at this than I am."

I nearly choked on the water I'd just bravely sipped when I realized he was being serious. I was tempted to drop kick him off the bed for saying somethin that stupid.

"Sorry to be the one to tell ya you're delusional, Grimm. He could never make me feel like you do." I leaned over, intendin to plant a solid kiss on his cheek, aiming for right above his beard, but then he turned his head and suddenly his hand was gripping the back of my neck and he had his lips on mine.

I gasped, unsure what to do. I mean, I knew what to do, but this was Grimm. My reaper had his mouth on mine.

I reiterated the *my* part of that thought as he took complete control.

I willingly let him have somethin I never pictured me givin someone ever again.

But again…this was Grimm. The man who told me less than five minutes ago that he wanted me whatever he could have me—which was majorly confused, undeniably fucked up, and forever being a smartass.

It was crazy to trust death with life, but I'd never trusted anyone more than I did him in that very moment. His skilled mouth coaxed mine to part, and then he had his skilled, silken tongue caressing mine.

I admit it took me longer than I'd have liked to reciprocate, because no woman wanted to miss a single second when it came to kissing this gorgeous man.

That tick in my chest turned into the rapid beating of a heart as I kissed him back. He tasted like the sweetest sugar, dissolving on my tongue like a drug.

We were in a rundown hospital, but we could have just as easily been standing on top of a mountain with fireworks goin off somewhere.

His hands didn't stray, and he didn't push for more.

I leaned into him and cupped his face, stroking the inverted cross I'd been eyeing since we met. His skin was so much softer than I would've thought. His beard stubble was rough on my palm.

It was *me* wanting more. I wasn't sure where that sudden urge came from, but it was vicious in its hunger, and carnal in its need to be sated. Maybe it was because I actually wanted him, or maybe it was simply one of those things that was always going to happen between us.

He pulled back before I could think about it too much with a grin on his face, keeping us nose to nose.

"Don't ever say you're not good at this again, you liar." I dropped my apple core on his lap and leaned back.

“That good, huh?” He shot the apple across the room, making a perfect score into the rusted sink. “That was just a sample.” He gave me a roguish smile it was impossible not to return.

I was well aware of that. Grimm just had a look about him. It was like a flashing red warning sign about that bad habit I’d mentioned earlier.

He was the kind of man who fucked you so good you thought of it every single day for weeks on end and replayed every second of it as you were foldin the laundry.

Maybe I was more screwed up than I thought. I didn’t know if it was abnormal to feel such a way after what happened to me, but *this*—having him look at me the way he was—it felt powerful and destructive. And *that* was preferable to that sick, weak, pathetic feeling that seemed like a parasite trying to plant itself in my brain.

"Here," he finally said, manipulating my body as if I were a porcelain doll so I was on my back with my head in his lap.

I felt an obvious hardness beneath my skull that was apparently goin to be the starved elephant in the room.

"We won't be here long, so we can talk later. You need to sleep now. "

I crossed my feet at the ankles and snuggled further into his hoodie.

I didn't feel tired, but I didn't feel like fallin off his bike because I got no sleep at all. I couldn't doze off like this, though.

"All I had was silence; I want to hear your voice." *It's my new favorite sound*, I silently added.

When the quiet stretched on, I didn't think he was inclined to indulge me. I might have been pushing, but I soon found myself with a small smile as he began tellin me about the hospital we were in.

With a gentle hand resting on my stomach, he spoke while looking down at me, and I looked right back at him with something lodged in my throat. Timing was said to be everything, and my reaper had come back into my life at just right the moment.

Face to face like this, everything became meaningless. I forgot where we were. Who I was no longer mattered when it felt like I was staring at myself, seeing something harsh and cold but full of blaze reflected back at me.

It's like time stopped and then reset with a countdown for somethin much larger than I could fathom just waitin to happen. His pretty, soulless hues were like a bottomless well, and he had no problem dragging me down, straight to the bottom where Tartarus waited.

When I finally started driftin off, it was with the thought that this was one bad habit I didn't want to ever be free of.

Chapter Ten

Arlen

When I woke, I saw sunlight.

It streamed through the dirty window and only made the room seem muggier than it had naturally become.

Grimm's voice came from right outside the door, and I knew he was on a cell. I sat up and tossed my legs over the side of the bed, and then stood.

Stretchin some kinks out, I pulled the hood down and went to the window. Standing on my tip toes, I peered out.

This wing of this hospital faced an old grocery store. I spotted an older man pushing a rusted shopping cart full of crates, and another man beside him with a bat.

"I thought ya'll took this city?" I asked, sensing Grimm back in the room. "I saw the Sigil on the sign."

"We saved this city. It was abandoned a little after I turned sixteen. I guess it wasn't big enough to have been salvaged. It took too many resources that could be used elsewhere."

"If it's abandoned what did ya'll save it from?"

He came up behind me and clamped his hands on either side of my waist, peering out the window. I tensed only a little, swallowing quietly. I wasn't expecting him to take his time with us, but this would still take getting used to.

"You see how old they are. All they're trying to do is live in comfort. They were being killed off, bodies left to rot in the open. Romero solved the problem."

I turned all the way around at that.

"The Savages care about the elderly?"

"The Savages want peace. Only, our version of it is more like anarchy. The elderly in Rivermouth don't give a shit. They just want to be left alone. Think of it as a retirement community. Those men are taking the crates of perishables and passing them out to others, courtesy of that man you know as the devil," he said with a smirk.

Now I was full on curious, but he had other ideas than me askin questions. He pulled my body into his, bringin us flush together and dropping his mouth to mine. This kiss was different to the first one. I could damn near taste his own desire on the tip of his tongue.

He slid his hands around to my ass and squeezed the cheeks. The second a groan left my mouth and I pressed further against him, he was pulling away.

"What was all that?" I breathlessly asked.

"I wanted to see something," he replied with a straight face.

Well, that was ominous. "What—"

A door slammed from somewhere, making my stomach jump.

Grimm's whole demeanor changed. One second he was right in front of me, and the next he was pushing his gun into my hand and movin away. The gun I'd forgotten about and didn't know how to use.

"Stay here," he commanded.

"You can't…leave me," I wound up sayin to myself as he disappeared in the blink of an eye.

Like hell I was stayin behind in this rinky-dink room. I slipped out into the hall, the sun allowing me to see everything but Grimm, and I couldn't hear him, either.

Damn, he was fast.

Chargin ahead, I jogged down the hall through a pair of double doors barely hanging on their hinges.

I popped out on somethin on an arched bridge, overlooking the floor below on either side. Straight ahead was another set of doors leading to another wing.

Voices below weren't what had drawn my full attention. The fact I was seeing Grimm in front of two men with that unmistakable V and snake tattoo was.

I saw only the men from that room, and I saw Grimm. They didn't know I was there, but I reckoned Grimm did.

One of the men moved too fast for my liking, and I didn't even think about what I was doing—I aimed the gun and pulled the trigger.

The pop was louder than I'd expected, and I missed. Both looked up like idiots. I'd barely blinked, and Grimm had one of their throats slit.

Blood went everywhere. I watched the man clutch at his neck, as if that could make it better. An odd sound came flying from his mouth.

A light thump from the opposite end of the hall had me looking away. Another man had just pulled open the doors, pausing when he saw me. He had hair as long as mine and had clearly ran to get this to point, as he was out of breath.

I wasn't a hundred percent certain he was with the men below, but he damn well wasn't with me, so I shot at him too. I felt the bullet leave the chamber this time and was prepared, expected the sound it made.

"For real?" I asked aloud when red spread across his chest, staining clean through his brown jacket. I'd been aimin for his head.

"Little bitch," I heard him gasp, crystal clear. When he ducked back through the door, I caught a glimpse of the V on his neck.

It all happened rather quickly—I'm talking in a span of three minutes or less. So where the fuck had Grimm vanished? There was no sign of him below, and there was only one body.

The man whose throat he'd slit was lying on the floor twitching. I wanted to yell out his name but had no idea how many of these men were in the building. I was too shit of a shot to take on multiple people, and I didn't know how many bullets I had left to try. If one of them had a gun of their own, I was screwed.

Oddly, I didn't feel afraid. I was pissed. Me and Grimm weren't supposed to be separated. With what he'd just told me about this town, I had a good feeling these fuckers had come here specifically for me.

Rushing across the bridge, I pushed through the rusted door the man I'd shot had just gone through. He was using the wall as support, trying to get away. I could've gone about my business and let him eventually fall to his knees, sufferin, but fuck that. I wanted him to meet death then and there.

"Let's see if I can get you dead this time," I muttered, following after him.

He looked over his shoulder at me and shook his head. “You don’t have to do this, little miss. I’m only doing as I was told.” He coughed, leaving a small dribble of blood on his cracked lower lip.

Little miss? I’m positive the word he used a minute ago was bitch. I glanced at his tattoo and couldn’t help but sneer. He was as pathetic as the others had been.

He stopped hobbling and leaned against the wall, huffin and puffin. I stepped right in his face, getting the eye contact I suddenly craved.

“Well, your shitty boss didn’t have to stick his dirty dick in me, but he must not have been thinkin with the right head.” I pressed the extended end of the gun to his temple and pulled the trigger. I saw the life leave his widened eyes as they looked straight back into mine.

I watched the blood and bone splatter on that filthy peelin wall, and the rush that gave me could only be described as euphoric.

I'd seen lives snatched away many times, but I had never been the one to send someone to the afterlife. If this was how Grimm felt, I could understand exactly why he liked his job so much.

That single thought of him had me hurrying away from my first fatality, runnin down the hall. At the far opposite end, something groaned. It sounded like rusted metal, and at least two voices followed right after.

Making a split decision, I veered toward a door that was half bent at the bottom, preventing it from opening any more than it was. I could see a semi-dark stairwell beyond and squeezed through it, knowing Grimm had been on the floor below this one.

I exited right out the door that led to the next floor, bouncing off an old wheelchair.

"Shit," I hissed, recovering as quickly as I could. "They're comin."

I hauled my ass to my feet and took off, away from the dead body Grimm had left behind.

The room I'd found myself in was circular and massive. I had no idea where to go. Grimm told me this place had everything from a chapel to a theater; I didn't know where he was, or if he was okay.

"Hey!" a voice called from behind me, carrying through the empty building. I heard the sound of footfalls, and poured on speed, dodging old medical equipment.

I swear I felt breath on my neck. Our footsteps sounded like a barrage of thunder coming from every direction at once.

To hell with this.

I darted through the next door on my right and stopped a few feet inside, whirling around just in time to get smacked into by the guy who'd been behind me.

I wasn't braced enough to take the hit, and he was too close to shoot. We went over the edge of the old in-ground pool I'd barely caught myself from falling into just a second ago.

Who the fuck designed this layout?

Naturally, the pool wasn't full, but there was enough murky rainwater that had come through the roof to coat the bottom so that whatever equipment had been tossed in was submerged. A drop was a drop, though, and this wasn't a kiddie's pool.

It hurt bad enough to knock the wind from my lungs. It smelled terribly, like rotten egg salad. I tried not to think about all the contamination and bacteria I'd just landed in.

I hit the grizzly bear of a man who'd tackled me in the head with the end of my gun as soon as I could steady myself enough to do so, albeit it wasn't a strong one, due to our new situation.

He cried out and lunged at me, grabbing hold of my wrists, sending me careening into a filing cabinet as we struggled. I internally cursed as my knee resonated with pain.

His intent was clearly to make me drop the gun. Mine was to shoot the fucker and not myself in the process. One shot rang out, hitting a decaying trolley. Another hit where bright blue graffiti was spray painted on the other end of the pool.

The tainted water was a hindrance to both of us. It soaked through my clothes; I tried my best to keep my mouth shut, not wanting to swallow a drop of it, when my feet were swept out from under me.

"You fucker!" I cried out, dropping the gun as my arm bent back at an unnatural angle.

It hit the black water with a depressing plop, sinking to a place I wouldn't be going to get it.

"Carter?"

“In here!” the man advancing towards me responded.

“I’m co—” Whatever his friend was gonna say ended abruptly, and a familiar voice let out a loud whoop immediately after.

There was another splash, and then Carter was gone. It took me a split second to realize the man with blood smeared on his face and down his arms was Grimm, currently gutting the man who’d tackled me.

I say gutting, because there was really no other way to describe what looked like a mini scythe slicing right up the middle of the man’s stomach. The skin made a crinkly sound as it was spread apart. The muscles in Grimm’s back and arms flexed from the strain of him dragging his curved blade upward, cutting through abdominal muscle and tissue.

Immediately, a smell much stronger than the stagnant water reached my nose, almost like a burning chemical.

Blood and somethin akin to grease ran down the man's front as intestines became exposed.

With a small grunt, Grimm all but kicked the man back off his blade. He went down but he wasn't dead yet. His body violently convulsed, making mini bubbles in the water.

"Ugh, that smell is—"

"Like roses!" a voice exclaimed from above.

I looked up and immediately found a pair of silver eyes.

"Cobra?"

"The magnificent," he beamed, holding a hand out to me.

I smiled back at him, glancing at Grimm, who was sloshing his way towards me.

He was covered in blood, corpse juice, and tainted water from head to steel toed boot, yet he looked damned good, in my opinion.

"Here," he said when he reached my side, hoisting me towards Cobra, who easily lifted me the rest of the way out of the pool.

Bless him for not mentioning the way I knew I smelled.

I was sat gently to the side so he could grab Grimm and one handedly help pull him out next. He wasn't breathin hard or nothin. I sat there feelin like a deflated balloon.

He looked down at me with a storm in his eyes. "Didn't I tell you to stay put?" he asked, pulling me off the dirty floor.

"I'm gonna go try and get a signal." Cobra was quick to interject, winking at me before making a hasty retreat. I only then noticed he had blood on his hands too, no doubt the result of that whoop I'd heard.

I stared at Grimm, doing another sweep to make sure he was really okay before shoving him in the shoulder. I put effort into it but he was like an immovable stone.

"You're a real dickhead, you know that? You can't hand someone a gun who doesn't know how to use it, and then poof into thin air."

"I didn't think you'd be that shitty of a shooter. You aim and pull the trigger Brat, preferably not to shoot me next time."

I swiped strands of filthy wet hair off my face and glared at him. "Well, I sure as hell can shoot at close range, and this shitty shooter was the distraction that saved your ungrateful self. Why would you leave me in the first place!? You can't do that. You're not allowed to leave me behind, Grimm!" I reckon from the sound of my voice, I was close to hysteria at this point.

I really didn't like this. Being such a hormonal mess was embarrasin enough, but doing it in front of him was a million times worse.

When it registered that he'd said somethin about me shootin him, my eyes went right to his arm that had the most blood on it.

I didn't see a bullet hole, but neither of the men he'd shot back at that shithole of a house had gaping holes from where'd he'd shot them.

"I-I shot you?" I rushed forward, feeling all over him, not thinkin this through at all, like I could find the wound and magically heal it with my hands alone.

He had too much blood and was too wet for me to tell what was what. When his body shook underneath me, I stopped and looked at his face to see if he was about to collapse.

"Cobra!" I yelled, a split second before I saw Grimm was laughin.

"Brat, you only grazed me," he explained when he got ahold of himself with the audacity to keep givin me that gorgeous smile of his that showed all his perfect teeth.

"What happened?" Cobra yelled, bustin through the door like a man on a mission.

"Your friend is a goddamn asshole," I answered, shoving past Grimm.

"Your gun's somewhere in that shitty water. Have fun fishin it out," I called back over my shoulder.

Chapter Eleven

Arlen

I didn't get to make a dramatic descent back to the room we'd been in and perform a miracle on my filthy clothes.

"Brat," Grimm called. He caught up to me, taking my hand firmly in his. "We need to have a private discussion." He was pullin me away without givin me much choice in the matter, much to Cobra's amusement.

“Talk later,” he mouthed at me just before I disappeared back into the stairwell I’d come out of.

“You’re leaving Cobra alone with those men lurkin around?” I hissed, trying to pull away. I was well prepared to go back and kick ass if need be. My muscles protested at that idea, but Cobra was the brother everyone wished they had—unless he was tryna get in your pants; then, he was somethin else entirely.

“You’re doing that pain in the ass thing,” Grimm said. He let my hand go and proceeded to scoop me up at the knees. “He can take care of himself, and actually hit his fucking target.” He slung me over his shoulder.

“What the hell are you doin? Put me down!” My voice echoed in the stairwell.

He ignored my protests and carried me back to the room we’d been in the night before. When he sat me down, he pushed the door shut and caged me between it and his body.

"I'm going to ask you a question, and I want you to answer me with the first thing that comes to mind. Can you do that, Brat?"

Nervous about where this was goin, I wanted to drop kick him in the balls. Trustin him nonetheless, I slowly nodded.

"What is it I want you to do?" he asked again.

"You want me to answer a question with the first thing I feel and nothin else." I repeated, and he nodded.

"The man you shot in the head, the one whose blood you haven't realized is on your face. How did it make you feel when pieces of his brain came out of his skull?"

"Good. Powerful. Alive," I tossed out all three.

"And how does that make you feel?"

"Scared, like I don't know myself anymore. That you won't like me this way."

He nodded again like he already knew this, and cupped my face.

I turned my cheek into his dirty, bloody palm, not caring it was adding to my filthy face.

"Your imperfections make you perfect, Brat. You're the most beautiful fucking thing I've ever seen. That darkness you've come to know…it has you feeling overwhelmed, but I promise you're not alone. I won't ever let you go."

Hadn't he told me he wasn't good at talkin? Every time he opened his mouth and said somethin meaningful, I fell for him a little more.

"Grimm. You are…"

"I'm basically a king, so by default, you're a queen."

"I was gonna say you're a goddamn idiot for not makin a move sooner than this. You've always been my dark, regal reaper," I teased, pulling his mouth down to mine.

He eagerly obliged, and I selfishly demanded more, attacking his mouth with mine, but he pulled away once again, leavin me keyed up with no relief—not to mention pissed off.

"I know you ain't celibate. I've heard you plenty. I can feel your dick is hard, so I know it's not me in general. So why can't you touch me?"

He gave me an inexpressive look and then turned away. "I want you to be sure," was his answer. I was seconds away from imploding.

"The men with the snake tattoos. How many?"

Now I was glad he couldn't see my facial expression when he asked that.

This was the question I was waitin on, the one I knew he'd eventually figure out. I reckoned that was where'd he'd gone off to.

He went to a bright orange duffel bag that must've recently been placed on the foamy bed, and unzipped it.

I could have pretended I didn't hear the question, or played stupid, but by the anger suddenly rollin off him in waves, he already knew, and just wanted me to verify it.

"He told me before I dropped him down an elevator shaft," he explained, responding to my silent thought.

I wanted him to know solely because I knew how this was goin to go. So I told the truth—the whole truth, and nothin but the truth, because that's what my Grimm wanted, and I needed to tell someone.

"It started with Vitus, but he didn't force me. I know that makes me sound like a cheap whore, but I thought it'd be over with if I just gave him what he wanted. Then his dad came in. His…uncle went next. The cousin."

I swallowed and looked down at the faded tile, feeling my stomach roll as I recounted it all inside my head. I took in a lungful of air and rushed through the next part.

"They took turns fuckin me in the ass while another one had his way with me in the front.

"I was held up between them, or on my side on that damn bed. I begged them to stop, and Arlen never begs. Arlen was strong and they took her away from me for no fuckin reason!

"They didn't care about the blood, or how bad it hurt, and Noah just stood there watchin so he could make good on his word, of all things."

"Why did they have to do that to me? Why am I the one who feels ashamed and dirty for what those sick assholes did?" I was sobbin into his chest by time I was done. He had his bloody arms around me and stood there like an immovable force, letting me get it all out of my system.

"Sorry I'm such a mess." I gave him a sheepish smile when I dared look back at him again.

"Don't ever apologize for this, Brat. If you can't cry on my bloody shoulder, what am I good for?" he joked.

I wondered if he knew he was the sole reason I was hangin on. He was supposed to be dead inside, yet here he was, making me feel alive.

He used his tongue and swiped a loose tear right off my face, and then stuck it in my mouth. I tasted my own filth and couldn't find a damn thing wrong with it. He bit down on the tip, not lettin up until I whimpered.

"What do you need from me, Brat?"

"I'm tired of seein their faces. I just want you to erase it. Make me feel better."

Taking my left leg, he hooked it over his hip and pressed his hard cock into my apex.

"This?"

"Yes," I groaned on a loose breath, grabbing his hips. I didn't give a damn where we were, that we had both just killed less than an hour ago, or that we were both coated in blood. Who was goin to judge us that mattered? If someone felt any type of way, that was their own damn problem.

My moral compass had begun to glitch. I couldn't find it in myself to give a damn about that, either. And was that really a bad thing?

Grimm tore away from me and lifted his shirt over his head, droppin it to the floor. My heart did some weird twist in my chest, and heat flared in my lower stomach as it erupted with flutterin.

His tattooed body was flawless. Every bump and ridge interconnected like a secret pathway. I took a step towards him, doing the same thing he'd done with my tank top, standing in front of him in nothing but my black bra and pants.

He undid the top button of his jeans, still moving away. As if there were an invisible choker wrapped around my neck, he became the master of my body, pulling me towards him with silent command.

"You're not ready for my kind of fucking, so you're going to have to sit your pretty ass on my lap and fuck me."

Oh, lawd. Between my legs clenched. I felt myself grow wet from his words full of dark promise of what would come later. I hadn't been with anyone aside from the pool boy and the men who'd used me.

I shook my head as if to free them from it. They wouldn't steal this from me; this choice was all my own. I wanted to give myself to this wicked man and let him do whatever he wanted to me.

He was more than likely right, though. I'd never been with a man like him. I responded to his promise by placing my hands on his solid chest and pushing him down on the bed. The duffel bag fell to the floor.

The devilish smile he graced me with made me want to repeat the move ten times more.

I worked my pants down that had become like a second skin since being wet, taking my underwear with them.

His eyes tracked over the fairy tattoo that spread down to where dark curls had begun to grow back due to me not havin a razor.

"I'm killing whoever did that," he said with no hint of humor. "You're beautiful, Brat." He reached for me, running his hands down my sides, around to the back of my thighs, cautious of the healin skin. "And that is the prettiest pussy I've ever seen."

He let me go, only to lower his jeans down, revealing a pair of black briefs. The outline of his cock was painfully obvious, and without a hint of shame, he pulled it out.

He was rock solid, tan just like rest of him, and more than a lil impressive. I peered up at him through half-mast lids.

I knew this was it, sealing the deal between us for good, and so did he. This wouldn't be a quick 'out of our system' spin cycle fuck.

His eyes were dark, like raven wings.

They were the type of darkness that wasn't dark. They were my rapture. There was no promise of dawn, only an endless midnight sky.

The danger held within them only allured me all the more, fanning a slow-burning desire and turning that spark between us into raging hellfire. I wanted him to burn me from the inside out and spread his ashes on my skin.

Straddling his lap, I gripped one shoulder with one hand and his smooth cock with the other, circling the head with my thumb.

"I got you." He gripped my hips, ensuring I wouldn't fall when I let his shoulder go.

"Grimm," I barely whispered, hovering over his tip. My hands gripped him harder than necessary as I fought against my paranoia. This was my reaper. He wouldn't use me like those men had. Grimm was my safety net. I had to get them out of my fuckin system.

"You don't have to do—goddamnn, Brat," he amended in a growly voice.

I took him inside me to the hilt, desperate to feel anything other than *them.*

I moaned loudly without embarrassment. He felt perfect; this burn was welcome. The pleasure and the pain had me clenching around him involuntarily.

He filled me entirely, stretching me as his cock slowly became embraced by my walls. I knew this wasn't his M.O. Grimm wanted control. I imagined he needed it to deal with the things that went on inside his own head. But he willingly sat there and gave it to me—somethin I didn't need.

I rolled my hips, tryna get a feel for this, and he flexed his hands. I did it again, watchin his face this time, and he glared slightly. His body was all tensed up, like iron.

"I'm not the kinda man you want to tease with your pussy. Fuck me hard, or I'll fuck you harder, and by time I'm done, you won't be able to walk in a straight line. Every crevice of your sexy ass body will be dripping with sweat, and you won't be able to remember your name because you were too busy screaming mine."

He gripped the back of my neck, slamming his mouth over mine, and lifted his hips, thrusting into me.

He bit down on my lower lip so hard he broke the skin. I cried out, and he slipped his tongue in.

His other hand was now firmly graspin my ass, guiding me up and down on his dick. He helped me find a rhythm, easing all the way up when I took over.

He caressed my back, ran his hands over my sides, and roughly took hold of my breasts—all as I rode him. The sounds comin from my mouth were unrecognizable.

"Harder," he demanded, with no change in his vocal inflection. With him soundin as normal as he always did, aside from his harsh grip, I thought I may have been goin about this the wrong way.

I straddled him a little more, taking him to the hilt every time I slid up then back down on his slickened cock. It felt too good. He felt so good it hurt.

He suddenly leaned back so he could watch me, loosely resting his palms back on my hips.

His eyes were saturated with raw desire, and it was all for me. I worked him faster, my breath coming in short puffs. The shitty bed was swayin in place, solely supported by the wall where paint-chips were steadily fallin away.

“That’s it,” he praised, his tone a lil more gravelly. “Fuck me, Brat. Use me. Take what you need.”

As if those were the words I’d needed to hear, that’s exactly what I did. Wrappin my arms around his neck, I rode him—hard.

Every moan, gasped breath, and whisper of his name from my mouth, and every occasional groan from him were like a balm. The way he was lookin at me, though, that was the salve—the numbing serum on scars invisible to the naked eye.

I felt whole, connected to him entirely—far beyond the physical.

Cupping his jaw, I traced the inverted cross beneath his eye. I wanted to commit everything about this moment, about him, to memory. His silky soft hair wasn't perfectly brushed back; he had growth to his beard, making him look more intense and rugged.

He smelled as good as he always did—he smelled of death. I felt the dried blood on his hands, saw the crimson stains on his face. I could still see his scythe ruthlessly slicing up the center of that man's stomach, smooth as butter, in my mind's clear lil eye.

Grimm was filthy, wicked down to his core, but he was the kind of filthy you wanted coating every fiber of your being, straight down to your bare bones. He used his bloody hands to keep me together when I wanted to break. He let me use his body to purge my heavy soul.

I wanted—needed—him to come inside me, needed him to replace everything those men took from me.

"Grimm," I moaned in his ear, trailing kisses down his neck. "Can you hurt me?"

"Give me your eyes." He tangled a hand in my hair and pulled so I was looking at him fully. "Now tell me what you want."

He made it impossible to glance away. I forced my lungs to constrict and retract. "I want you to hurt me." My voice was so clear, so steady in comparison to how I felt right then, like a tickin bomb that wouldn't be diffused unless it detonated. And only he could disarm me.

"I can make it hurt very, *very* fucking good, Brat." He pulled out and flipped us around, not so gently easin me down so the foamy mattress cushioned my back. Being on top of him was great, but him standing above me between my parted legs made me feel twice as powerful.

It was all in his eyes. If I told this man to get down and eat me, I knew he'd have every inch of his silken tongue inside my pussy.

"You sure you want this?" He asked the question as a means to give me a warning.

"I need it."

"I'll go easy this time."

I wanted to tell him I didn't want easy, but when my mouth opened, a gasp spilled out. He slammed inside me, purposely placin his hands on the raw, tender flesh of my thighs.

There were no pretenses after that. He squeezed, adding pressure, makin the sore skin feel like it was on fire. I whimpered, liftin my hips to take him deeper. His cock hit somethin inside me I wasn't aware existed.

"More," I demanded.

He watched me closely and dug the pads of his fingers into the same spot, beginning to knead the flesh. It did hurt, in the best fuckin way possible. I bit the corner of my lower lip, and my pussy clenched around his cock.

"Too fucking tight," I heard him say beneath his breath, picking up his pace.

The bed sounded like it was going to give out at any second. I felt a familiar pressure rapidly building, and reached for him. He instantly lurched down, giving me his tongue.

Meeting his solid thrusts took stamina I didn't have, so I attempted to take him deeper inside me, clawing his back and pulling him forward. I wanted him to tear me open and make me bleed.

I never got to ask that of him. He knew what was about to occur before I did. I'm certain it was him who made it happen.

"Damn Brat, you're gonna come," his gravelly voice nearly groaned. He moved to my neck, suckling on the juncture above my shoulder, and then he bit down. I think he broke through skin, but I couldn't focus.

Endorphins mixed with pain and I didn't know which one felt better.

Grimm's name hung in the air, spillin from my lungs like a chanted prayer. He was right.

I never knew it just how good it could hurt, not until him. My pussy clamped down on his cock as heat shot through my veins, makin me damn near convulse.

He kept goin. When he was right on the brink of his own release, he attempted to pull out. I locked my legs around him a lil tighter, digging my nails into his back so hard I felt his skin beneath them.

"Brat—"

"No," I breathed, refusing to let go.

"Fuck," he cursed, tensing in my arms. I pressed down, making sure I felt every twitch of his dick and as much of his come spurting inside me as I could. I held him close, never wanting to let go.

Chapter Twelve

Arlen

I wasn't sorry about what I'd done, but I didn't expect Grimm to feel the same way.

I admit I was confused when I dared look him in the eye again and saw his signature dark stare—the one that gave nothin away.

I'd been expecting to see anger, at the very least. I mean, I'd just trapped his swimmers inside me, and he didn't know I was on a contraceptive.

Feelin something wet under my fingertips, I drew my hands around, letting out a soft gasp when I saw blood.

"I'm sorry, Grimm, I wasn't tryna hurt you."

"Hurt me? Brat, if that's your definition of hurting me, by all means, fuck me up," he laughed softly.

"That might scar." I pointed out with more than a hint of concern, tryna turn him around so I could see the damage.

Grabbing my hand, he captured my bloody fingertips on his soft lips. Keeping eye contact, he sucked them into his mouth, right down to the knuckle, cleaning them with his tongue.

"You're so dirty," I laughed.

"Babygirl, this is me being clean." He gave me a lil smirk and stepped back, taking his semi-hard cock with him.

"I want you to scar me, make me bleed. Use me anytime you want. I'll be doing the same to you soon enough."

I wanted him to do that right that second, even as I sat there with burnin skin, an achin, swollen pussy, and his come drippin between my wide open legs.

But I knew there was too much we hadn't discussed. Actually, we hadn't spoken about a damn thing aside from cementin in the fact that I was his and he was mine. Not that it was much of a discussion, considerin I'd been his from the very day he put me in a chokehold upon our first meeting.

"We should probably…discuss all the stuff that needs discussing," I said. "Like me bein on birth control, not that you seem to concerned. Should I be worried about that? Is this a typical thing you do? Cause you sure won't be anymore, so if there's some pretty lil thing waitin for you at home with her heart on her sleeve, let me know. I'll make sure she and I have a clear understandin of who the hell you belong to."

Not givin me an immediate response, Grimm grabbed the duffel bag we'd knocked on the floor and sat it on the bed.

"You've been my main priority since you went missing. If you want me to say that I didn't shove my dick down someone's throat, I'd be lying to you. But none of those bitches are around anymore, and you know what happened to them."

He went back to being quiet after that, but I could tell he had more to say. I let him work it out in his head, not pushin. He'd been so open with me, I couldn't be upset. Grimm wasn't a talkative man. I would accept this for the simple fact that there wasn't a single thing about him I wanted to change.

I took the small bundle of fresh clothes Cobra had had the foresight to bring, and watched him tear open a packet of wet wipes.

He shook one out and stepped between my legs, gently wiping my face clean.

The thin piece of cotton was cool and smelled like lavender. I shut my eyes, letting him work, keeping them closed when he began to speak.

"You make me feel shit I've never felt before, want things I didn't think I'd want. I fucking hated that when I first met you.

Why do you think I tossed your ass right back to the cannibal who was chasing you?" He began rubbing down my arms next.

"You were right. Maybe you ain't so good at this," I quipped, opening my eyes. "You also helped hold a damn machete on top of my head, but we can just sweep that under the rug."

"I was ready to kill you to prevent this. Look at us now, though, destined to be epically fucked up," he joked, laughing beneath his breath.

"I'm gonna have to shut you down, because I'm one hundred percent sound of mind," I deadpanned.

He tossed another wipe down and gave me a serious look.

"I'm not a poet, Brat. I can't give you long, drawn out exclamations drenched in honey.

Words always fade away, and eventually mean nothing. I let my actions speak for me."

Cue a mental eye-roll. "I know all this, Grimm. I get you."

"You get me, huh?" he asked, wiping his dick off and then removing his old pants completely to pull on a fresh pair with clean briefs. "Then you wouldn't have tried to skin me alive, you little hellion." He knelt, swapping socks and then re-lacing his boots. "I wasn't going to pull out; I was trying to switch positions. I know he was giving you a pill. Now, get dressed, because I do need to have a conversation with you about a few things, Noah included."

"Then what?" I asked, pulling the fresh black tank top over my head.

"I think you know what," he answered.

And I did, which is why when he asked me earlier, I'd told him everything, why I made sure I had the guts big enough to end someone's life. I wanted every single one of those men dead, especially Noah. I wanted him down on his knees, weeping for mercy.

He'd survived far too long.

But was I savage enough to do somethin like that over and over again? Realizing I'd gone off on a mini mental tangent and Grimm was now sliding my new shorts up my legs himself, I began tryna explain.

"I've never felt like this before. I'm not real sure how to deal with it…hate, anger, the pain. It's never-ending. I feel stuck in reverse, but I swear I'm trying to keep movin forward."

"You're the only thing groundin me right now. I'm not ashamed to admit that." I pulled my stretchy shorts the rest of the way up and did the top button.

Grimm began tying my left boot as soon as I had it on, clearly in a hurry to get on with this whole shebang.

"I won't tell you to get the fuck over it, but I am going to get you through it. I'm yours, Brat. You don't need to worry, you don't have to hide. Trust me to take care of you. I’ll be whatever you need, as long you don’t let those fuckers be the reason you lose your soul.”

He stood and took hold of my face, his gaze searching for somethin he must’ve found, cause he smiled so beautifully I think my heart stopped all over again. “You and I are going to have so much fun together.” He pressed a possessive kiss on my slightly parted lips, resting his forehead on mine. “Hold onto your hatred, hold onto the pain and the rage. I’m going to show you how fucking beautiful it all is."

I didn’t have any idea on how to take that promise. Cause that’s what it was—a dark promise, maybe even a sworn oath.

But I was more than ready to find out.

Part Two

She who walks the floors of hell finds the key to the gates of her own Heaven buried there like a seed.

–SEGOVIA AMIL–

Chapter Thirteen

Grimm

I shined the light down on his broken body.

His upper half was bent back so far the exposed portion of his skull nearly touched his ass.

Cobra's impressed whistle echoed down the old shaft. He knew I'd rather go right in for a kill than drag anything out. The man lying scalped and broken on the top of the old elevator said otherwise.

"Damn, Grimmy. What the fuck did he say? This isn't yo style."

"You have a style?" Brat asked, still curiously peering over the ledge.

"Beth told him my name," I said.

"My sister?" Brat whirled around, glancing between us.

Having a third sense that her clumsy ass would misstep right down the shaft, I pulled her away from it.

Cobra stepped back as well, crossing his arms with furrowed brows. "Arlen's sister," he pointed at Brat, "told one of Vance's men your name? Why? How the fuck is she still running those loose pussy lips of hers?" He glanced at Brat again. "I do mean that offensively, by the way. Your sister is a—"

"Cum-hoarder, I know. But what are ya'll talkin about? How would she know these snake dudes, much less talk to em? Romero had her locked away."

I stepped back and leaned against the wall, pulling her into my side.

"In light of recent events, I have a pretty good hunch Beth hasn't been locked up for some time. The acolyte watching over her is the only one allowed in and out of the freezer where she's supposed to be being kept.

"Look what just happened a few months ago—our own fucking informants were turning from the inside. Ask yourself why, and then take into account Beth just happened to come around when that crazy bitch, Tiffany, did. She spontaneously ran away, making it out of The Kingdom, and Noah's working with Romero out of the kindness of his heart?"

"No one with even a quarter of a brain would fuck with the Savages. Yet, now these Venom fucks are involved. Noah isn't controlling them, so that tells us someone they feel is just as big as Romero is. And they have to be selling a pretty convincing dream."

I waited for them to catch on; it only took Cobra a minute.

"Well, fuck. Do you think Rome knows?"

"Knows that he could never trust Noah? Yes, no one is fucking trusting Noah. Does Rome know Venom is involved? No, me and you didn't even know that, which means it's on the DL."

Cobra ran his hands through his hair, letting out a deep breath. "So the coach is throwing a tantrum because he just lost his QB?" He spoke in code, shooting a subtle glance at Brat, saying all I needed to know without saying a word.

"Hold up a sec. Why would my father do any sort of business with Noah or the…snake dudes? What they could possibly offer him?" Brat asked.

She'd caught onto a good gist of what I was saying, but not the most important parts.

"It's a long story. I'll tell you on the road."

"I'll go find a signal to call Rome. You two get your shit," Cobra said, already zipping down the hall. "Meet me in the old chapel!"

Brat stared up at me with an expectant look on her face. She wanted answers to all the questions I knew she had, and I didn't want her to know about any of this. Now, I understood why Rome had kept so much from my sister. The truths, the lies, and the secrets all had the ability to destroy in the right hands.

I wasn't him, though. And Brat wasn't Cali. We were our own people. This relationship was just me and her. She hadn't held anything back from me, and I was going to give her the same benefit. Ignoring our reality wouldn't bury or erase it.

I reminded myself she'd blown someone's brains out, watched me gut someone, and made me come like a little fucking boy all within the past few hours. Without giving her a warning, I reached out and grabbed her by the throat.

Her small gasp of surprise was the only emotion she showed.

Forcing her to walk backward, I made her stand right on the edge of the old elevator shaft.

If I dropped her, she would die, or break majority of the bones in her supple little body.

Keeping my grip as it was, I waited for her to yell, delving straight down the front of her shorts with my other hand, sliding her back a little more. Now, the back half of her boot was over the ledge.

I pushed two fingers inside her tight cunt, and she moaned. I began to pump them in and out, ignoring how hard my dick was, how fucking beautiful she was, and I waited.

I waited for her to demand I let her go, tell me I was a sick psycho, scream, cry—show any sign that this was all some mental fluke.

I'd want her all the same, but maybe it wouldn't be to this extent. Every time I fucking looked at her, I was ready to get down on my knees and worship at her alter.

She made me feel, made me care, laugh, joke.

I made promises to keep her safe and make her strong, show her how beautiful hell was.

She said I kept her grounded. Even if this were inevitable, it was happening faster than I thought it would.

She humanized me, and to some people that was no big deal, but when you spent damn near nineteen years dehumanized, killing every women you fucked or didn't fuck for sport, it was unnerving.

It was having all my don't give a fucks come back at once in the form of a woman.

Whose bright idea was it to give death the seed of life? Didn't they know what I'd do to her? Make her a sinner. Be like my brother and think of myself as a king. Crown her my queen of everything dark and dead.

The intense fucking sunlight in her eyes was a siren's song that would tempt the strongest man.

I wanted to fuck her again and again until a red river was flowing from between her juicy thighs.

"Grimm." She swallowed audibly, flooding my fingers with her pussy's arousal, as if she'd heard my last thought aloud, getting more turned on the harsher my grip got.

I could end this all right now and let her go, try and go back to how my life was before. I couldn't, though. Swinging her away from the ledge, I pressed her into the wall, shoving her shorts down far enough that I could get my dick inside her.

She fumbled with the top button on my jeans, gripping my cast-iron dick and damn near forcing it inside all on her own. I knew she was sore from just twenty minutes ago, and how rough this would be with a wall of peeling paint and half spread legs to accommodate my size. I slammed in to the hilt.

My balls were already lifting to spill. I'd found heaven, and it was inside her pussy.

She clenched around me, grabbed my hair, and pulled.

I fought the urge to come like a little bitch and fucked her like she was a whore.

She began moaning so loud she could've woken the man with the missing scalp lying on top of the elevator just a few feet away from us.

I belatedly realized she was saying my name. I usually hated that shit, but Brat could do no wrong. It was a quick, thrusting in and out, pounding my balls into her cunt hard and fast type of fuck. She came when I bit down on the side of her neck and slammed her into the wall, like the good little pain-slut she was becoming.

I came with a low grunt, pumping every drop of my come into her. She shuddered against me, breathing heavily.

"Damn, we should have been doin this a long time ago."

She smiled up at me, and my chest constricted so goddamn hard it almost hurt.

The advice I'd been given echoed in my head—when you know, you know.

"I like that you're filthy. I like that you're mine." She smiled again, planting a kiss right at the corner of my mouth.

Maybe I should have done this shit a long time ago, but then we wouldn't be who we were right this second. My fucking emotions didn't know whether to be up or down. I stared at her with my usual mask in place. Maybe I'd gone crazy, maybe I was fucking weak, but I could never set her free.

I think she got it wrong, because I felt like she'd just grounded me—like an anchor wrapped around my balls. Looking at her like this, I found what I'd been searching for but saw it from a different angle. It wasn't sunlight I was seeing at all.

Fuck Romero for always being right.

Her halo was broken, but there was brimstone burning in her eyes. Her hatred was beautiful.

I'd give her a crown forged of blood and bone from every motherfucker who'd laid a hand on what was mine.

I hoped she was ready to paint some shit red. We weren't going home until their bodies were at our feet.

Chapter Fourteen

Arlen

Assume the worst. Expect it to be even worse than that.

That's how I was going to think of all the things Dad could've done. Grimm said he'd tell me on the road, and I was patient enough to wait. Besides, I wasn't really excited to know how much shit Dad had started. Cobra's ridiculous code talk hadn't gone over my head. I knew full well what a coach and quarterback was.

I wasn't surprised he'd had help from over the wall, either—just who it was helping him. Why Noah? What role did Romero have in it?

They were questions I didn't even know if I wanted the answers to, but couldn't afford to be naïve about.

I followed behind Grimm with a bottle of water, munching on a pack of old saltine crackers he'd procured for me out the duffel after a pee break. I had his atomic bag on my back, the straps tightened so it wasn't slouchy. I was assuming we were about to head out; course, Grimm was being mysterious and didn't explain it, but he'd gathered up our minimal supplies, shoving them in the bag I now carried, so that was my guess.

The sun was starting to set, giving the old hospital a creepy aesthetic. We found the chapel easily enough.

Cobra hopped up from an overturned rotten pew the moment he saw us.

"They're here. Talk fast before I lose my signal again," he said into a cellphone that looked more like a giant walkie-talkie with a long antenna. I hadn't seen one of those in ages, but I'd heard they got reception best in situations like these.

"I'm sending some acolytes to Plymouth. Go to Lucy's and she'll have a lead waiting along with them." Romero's voice crackled over the line, and it didn't take a magician to figure out he was pissed.

"From there, you do what you have to do, but I want Noah alive. I'm gonna piss on him as he bleeds out like a fucking pig over a fire."

"I can feel the brotherly love from here," Cobra joked.

"Are you sure about this?" Grimm asked.

"Don't ask me stupidass questions, and Arlen, don't fucking die."

"Wasn't plannin to, fucker," I muttered.

"Smartass—" His voice cut off. I thought the line had gone dead, some secret blessin, but there were muffles in the background.

"Have fun, Arlen! I'll be here, round, depressed, and cheering you on." Cali's voice boomed through the speaker loud and clear, making me smile.

"Call me when you get to Plymouth," Romero snapped. The phone made an elongated beep and then cut off.

"Let's go," Grimm said, taking me by the hand.

"Where exactly are we goin, and why will there be acolytes?"

"You know where we're going. We're going to kill shit, girl. And wherever that is, Rome is sending us some manpower," Cobra answered.

The surrealism of the situation was quick to sink into my mind. We were really doin this. I had wished it, I had told Grimm, and now it was happenin.

"Who has a pre-game conversation before they go to kill people?" I asked, tryna distract myself from my inner thoughts as we made our back towards the parking deck.

"People getting ready for a game, and you're on the winning team now, sis," Cobra grinned.

"Sis?" I asked. "So I'm no longer the random chick who was probably going to die?"

I was joking; we'd long surpassed that, but he'd said somethin along the lines of that to me upon the first kill I'd seen them do inside an old church. Such good times.

I could see he was legit excited about doin this, to the point the man was nearly bouncing on his toes.

"How does Romero know we'll need acolytes for…whatever you just said?"

"Romero is always twelve steps ahead, and never shows his full hand. He more than likely knows exactly what's going on by now, has a bloodbath pile accumulating, and is waiting on us to make our move," Grimm said.

"Sounds much too stressful. Speakin of, how's the baby?"

"Baby S is fine," Grimm answered.

Lawd, I didn't think the whole baby S, a.k.a., baby Savage would stick. That kid was going to be a ruthless little fucker.

A loud bang echoed from somewhere in the building. We stopped and looked at one another, none of us saying a word.

Then, at the same damn time, Cobra and Grimm each pointed in the direction behind us. Clearly, they'd heard somethin extra that I couldn't.

"They probably had a look out, and seeing as how not a single one of them exited this hospital, he went for help," Cobra said quietly.

"Venom," Grimm explained at my look of confusion. "The name of the gang with snake tattoos."

"For real? That's what they came up with? Venom is a really stupid fuckin name," I quipped.

"Yeah," Grimm laughed. "It is."

"You ready?" Cobra asked me suddenly.

"For what?" I asked at the same time Grimm said, "Take this," and passed me a pearl white switch blade he'd just removed from one of his back pockets.

"We're gonna take this staircase on the next left, go down the stairs, exit on the next level, go down the hall, circle back up, and haul ass to the parking garage," Cobra explained.

I had to walk myself through what he was saying twice in my head before I had it down pat. How the hell did they all think on their feet so fast?

"Why the hell would we run? I thought the Savages didn't get scared?"

"Excuse the fuck out of me, but it was to keep *you* safe, princess," Cobra drawled.

We entered the staircase and I wound up sandwiched between them, clearly on purpose.

"Why does Noah want me so badly?" I asked as we exited onto the next floor.

"Because he has a god complex," Cobra snorted, stepping through the open doorway that led to the next level.

"The same reason he was giving you those pills," Grimm answered.

I ain't know what he meant by that, and didn't get a chance to ask.

A woman's short scream blasted through the air. It was so unexpected, I almost fell over my own two feet. If we'd gone left, it came from the right. It was followed by a door slamming.

"Keep moving." Grimm nudged my lower back. "They might not be here for you after all."

What the hell? "So those fuckers are gonna hurt some other woman, and we're gonna keep going about our business?" I protested and tried to stop walkin, but Grimm was right at my back preventin me from doing so.

"There aren't any heroes here, sis. Don't go trying to change that," Cobra said, siding with Grimm, of course.

I didn't want to be a goddamn hero; I wanted to slit their fuckin throats open. I wanted to see how they liked havin the tides turned on them. I condemned every single one of those bastards by association.

They made me suffer, and laid me to ruin. They took pride in my pain, and took what didn't belong to them. It was because of them that I felt dead inside.

I never fuckin wanted this. I didn't ask to be forsaken and left to crash in the dark. But that's where I was now. Grimm wanted me to embrace my hatred, pain, and rage. Well, this was me doin just that. I could feel it pumpin through my veins like a bittersweet madness.

I stood and planted myself between my boys.

"They made a mess of me. They need to pay for their sins and atone with flesh and bone."

It was silent for all of five seconds.

"Well then, I can't argue with that excellent point," Cobra humphed, his demeanor swiftly changin. "She wants to play, Grimmy."

Grimm ignored him entirely, focusing solely on me, seeing everything I wasn't saying aloud. "I'm not going to try and stop you. If this is what you want, let the red crusade begin." He stepped back and opened the door we'd just come through.

"You won't see me, but I'll always be right behind you." He nodded down the stairwell. "Go, you're running out of time."

Knowing his words were full of promise, I darted through the doorway, planting a quick kiss on his cheek on my way past.

I stood on the landing for a few seconds, tryna get my bearings. When I glanced back, Grimm and Cobra were nowhere to be seen.

They would know just where to go. Unlike me, those two were well seasoned hunters.

Knowledgeable of how large this damn hospital was thanks to Grimm, they could've been anywhere. But as if I had some internal compass, I knew exactly which way to head.

I began making my way down the stairs, oddly thinking of Ma as I did. What would she say if she knew I was seconds away from making peace with the demon crawling up my spine like a black widow eager to spread its venom through my veins?

What would she think of me now that I'd kissed death and liked it?

She'd probably preach to me and tell me to get down and pray, not understandin it was too late. There was no redemption for the wicked.

I had nothin to repent for.

I wouldn't have any regrets.

I'm sorry Father, for I no longer give a shit.

Chapter Fifteen

Arlen

It didn't take me long to find her.

It would seem lady luck was on my side for once, because I saw them before they saw me.

The girl, who actually looked older than me, had just rounded the corner.

I stepped back into a doorway, trying to ignore the damn awful smell emanating from behind me. Whatever was inside the room had been rotting for a while now.

This situation was nothin like mine, seein as I'd been chained up in an old barn, but I still couldn't help but think of myself as I watched the dark haired girl make her way in my direction. The man behind her was large, but my height, and his hair looked white, but he wasn't old.

While I didn't want to go swoopin in like a white knight, I wouldn't forget it was Cali who saved me when she could so easily have left me behind. I was never supposed to have made it this far.

Engagin the switchblade Grimm had given me, I saw the white handle had an intricate floral design, and briefly smiled. He'd brought it for me. The blade looked like one sharp point, bout ten centimeters long, making the whole thing around twenty one centimeters.

The girl zipped on right past me, and I readied myself. I wasn't sure if she saw me standin there. I didn't have a plan, aside from making sure he stopped breathin.

Before he could pass, too, I kicked the old wheelchair I'd been eyeing right at him. It worked; he nearly tripped.

In the end, looking down was what cost him. By time he looked up again, I was in his face and the blade was finding a home right in his left eye.

I couldn't even be surprised at myself for moving in so swiftly with no hesitation. It felt too natural. I made sure my thrust was strong. I needed to penetrate his cranial cavity so the blade could efficiently reach the brain. That was basic science.

What I wasn't expectin was the eye to be so weak. There was a lil wet popping sound as the blade went right into the center, as if I were slicing a piece of smooth, red velvet, the kind with that sweet tangy icing on top.

Blood didn't go in any particular direction; it just seemed to spray out, like a hydrant. The round orb squished, and I damn near gagged.

His scream was so loud, my eardrum suffered, ringing in response.

The girl, who I thought had kept runnin, was suddenly beside me, kickin the man square in the stomach. He couldn't find his balance, resulting in him falling backward, his eye socket sliding off my knife.

The eye was gone, shoved backward somewhere in his skull. A pit had taken its place, blood flowing down the man's face in streaks of diluted burgundy.

Unfortunately, the fucker didn't drop dead like he would've if this were a slasher film.

The girl charged and jumped on him like a damn banshee. He went down, tripping over the wheel of the decaying wheelchair, landing flat on his back, still screaming about his eye.

In nothing but a sky blue skirt, she sat right on his head, using all her strength to keep him pinned on the dirty hospital floor.

"Kill him!" she yelled over her shoulder at me.

Not havin to be told twice, I took her initiative and straddled his beer belly, plantin my knees on either side of his waist.

Adjusting my grip on the slippery handle, I did what I'd said I was goin to, driving it through the center of his throat, pulling it back out and slicing to the left, then the right, making sure I got the jugular and all the extra sensitive parts, making sure death was his end result.

There was a loud whoosh of air and a red blob spilled from his mouth. His body twitched like I'd electrocuted him. Blood was goin everywhere, completely ruinin the girl's bright blue skater skirt. Why the hell she was wearing that in the first place was beyond my understandin.

Her whole outfit was. Looking cute while travelling through the Badlands didn't seem all that important to me. Her top was tight, black and floral, a halter like bodysuit.

She had shiny plum polish on her fingers, a few tattoos on her arms, and a Cruella Deville type thing going on with her long hair.

"Well, what do we have here? Room for one more?" Cobra asked, stepping through the door I'd come through with Grimm and two others right behind him.

"What the fuck are you doing?" Grimm wrapped an arm around my middle, lifting me off the man's belly. For real? He was jealous of a dead guy?

"Me? What happened to you two being *right* behind me?"

"They happened," he answered, jerking his head in the direction of the two people behind them.

"They used our skill-set as their cover against the other two snack head fuckers," Cobra added, staring at the brunette's bloody legs longer than was acceptable. "Damn, sis. You did that?" He gave me a bright smile, gesturing to the man's face.

"That's nothin." I shrugged, trying to stay modest.

"You didn't have to filet his neck, Brat." Grimm said. His expression was blank, but there was a prideful look in his eyes that made me smile. "Come on, we can clean you up when we stop again."

"Is there blood on my face?" I lifted my hands up to check.

"No, but if you touch it with those, there will be," he said, grabbing my left wrist and starting forward.

"I'm Katya, but go by Kat," the dark haired girl said, steppin right into our path. She had a non-English lisp, and a small gap between her two front teeth.

"That's Blue and Parker." She gestured to her companions. The woman, Blue, actually had bold blue hair and could've been a pin-up girl in another life, and Parker had blonde dreadlocks with huge black gauges in his ears.

It was such an odd combination of people.

“We don’t have time for this.” Grimm kept walking, forcing Katya to step aside.

“Never say the Savages haven’t done the world an act of kindness,” Cobra said, giving a two finger salute and falling in step beside me.

We went right past the room with the horrible smell coming from beneath the door. I knew whatever or whoever was inside was dead, and had no desire to find out how much worse that smell was with no barrier between us.

The only people I gave a damn about were either right beside me, or hours away in a compound somewhere—so sucks for whoever the hell that person was who had to die in an abandoned shithole.

The group followed, not making a sound. Cobra and Grimm must not have thought them a threat, or they’d all be dead, and there was no way in hell they’d let them walk behind us.

“So what’s the deal with you guys? I mean, what are ya’ll doin in here?” I asked after a minute or two.

I’d just killed a man with Katya; it seemed kind of wrong not to say anything at all.

“Those freaks with the snake tattoos are all over the city,” Blue said.

“We were just making our way through, paying them no attention. They cornered our group off—we got away and they found us again. There used to be seven of us,” Katya added.

She didn’t seem torn up about the people lost, which reverted back to the old adage: safety in numbers. The Venom took out four of them, just because. That seemed to be a thing in the Badlands. It was survival of the worst. A human eat human world. There was no place for morals here. There was no law. The only rule out here if you wanted to live was simple: don’t have any rules.

The silence had awkwardness settling between our two trios as we headed in the same direction.

I wanted to keep them with us simply for the fact that they didn't seem outwardly evil. They were just strangers who wanted to survive. Didn't we all? My judgment of character hadn't let me down thus far.

I waited for Grimm to tell them they needed to go a separate direction—he didn't.

He and Cobra shared a look, doing the brotherly bond thing they always seemed to do.

The sun was nearly gone, leaving only faint light to pave our path to the parking deck.

We passed a body slumped against the wall with a long metal pole—I assumed a piece of an old hospital bed—jammed through the bottom of his jaw. His fixed eyes watched us pass him by.

On a staircase was another body with no visible marks; his head was facing an unnatural direction. I knew Grimm was responsible for that one.

He truly lived up to his personification. Death could be swift, fast, and something you never saw coming. That was Grimm.

His gaze was focused on the path ahead of us, no doubt in his own head, being his usual quiet self as he planned the journey of mass destruction we were about to embark on. I studied his side profile, feelin familiar warmth in my chest that came from looking at his handsome self.

I know he was supposed to be this unfeeling, cold, cruel man, but there was a heart in there somewhere. He showed me that time and time again. It was dark and diabolic, just like the man who carried it, but it was still a heart. I had every intention of owning it fully and completely. I knew it would take work. It could be said we were just two strangers with the same hunger: to feel loved, to feel a lil less lonely, to feel anything at all other than numb.

Hell, I didn't even know this man's real name, but the way I felt about him, I couldn't care less.

And that was really what it came down to, because I felt as if I'd known Grimm for a thousand lifetimes and was just now findin him again—like my twin flame. He was mine, I was his, and this hell was ours.

"What?" Grimm asked, glancing at me from the corner of his eye.

"Just thinkin." I laid my head on his shoulder and hid another smile.

Cobra, clearly feeling left out, hooked his arm through mine on the other side as we went down the last hall to the parking deck staircase.

Who'd have thought lil ol me would be in the shittiest of situations, again, but able to smile and laugh as dead bodies piled up by the hour? I'd killed two men, and had never felt stronger. I had my reaper to thank for that.

I had a man I considered a brother back.

I felt adrenalized. This new me wasn't so bad after all; seemed she got shit done.

Chapter Sixteen

Arlen

I was a bit surprised Grimm's Harley was fine, as was the 4x4 muscle car sitting beside it with a giant metal bar across its grill.

They sat in the back corner of parking deck C in perfect condition.

"The engines are going to draw them to us like flies on shit," Cobra pointed out, leaning on the hood of his car.

"How big is this group? Are they like the Savages?" I asked.

"No one can top what Romero built, but even ten people is ten bodies that need dealt with. I'm going to go out on a limb here and say there's at least that many, since little Blue," he stopped and pointed at the trio standing a lil ways away from us lookin completely at odds, "already told us they're all over the city. They're so desperate to get their hands on you that they invaded one of our territories. I don't think we're going to amicably talk our way out of this," Cobra said.

"Negotiating is for pussies." Grimm finally spoke up, placing a now empty gas can into Cobra's trunk. "I don't negotiate, I send people to an early grave." He walked behind me and slid the bag off my back, casually tossing it in Cobra's backseat in exchange for another he secured on the back of his Harley.

"Well, we need to get to Plymouth. So let's head out and take different routes. That'll make them go two separate directions. They won't bother us once we leave this city."

"The Venom is nothing but a group of boys trying to play in a league of men. This is a safety zone for them. Romero won't bring a bloodbath here, not with all the old crabs that could get caught in the crossfire. We both know there are acolytes lurking beyond Rivermouth, waiting to take them out," Cobra explained.

"So you go left and I go right, and then we meet in the middle? That's all you had to say," Grimm replied.

Cobra sighed, shaking his head. "You three! Get in the damn car," he called to Katya and her friends.

"You're going to take us with you?" Blue asked, sounding as surprised as I felt.

"Thank your friend with the bloody thighs and perfect ass. She sat on a man's face so sis could dig a knife in his throat. That bought your ride out the city."

There was so much wrong with his sentence I didn't know where to begin.

"Is it any safer to go with someone like him? He's a Savage," Parker whispered, not as quietly as he should have.

He had a good point, considerin. But I still didn't appreciate his prejudice.

"He offered ya'll a ride. Haven't you ever heard the saying don't look a gift horse in the mouth or somethin? Don't be a prejudiced dick. You don't know him, so get in the car, or get the hell out of the way."

Cobra thanked me with a bright smile, climbing into his driver's seat.

"Or something?" Grimm laughed, guiding me to his bike. He climbed on and waited for me to do the same.

"My hands are dirty."

"Your hands are bloody, and I think that's sexy. If we didn't have somewhere to be, I'd sit you on my bike and spend the next few hours doing the same to your pussy."

"Da-yum," Cobra laughed, cause, of course, he heard every word of that.

Grimm needed to dirty talk twenty-four seven, I'd realized. The thought of fuckin this magnificent man in front of an audience was more than a little temptin, but I'd rather do it somewhere we might not die as we were coming.

I grabbed his shoulder and climbed behind him, wrapping my arms tightly around his middle, breathin in his spicy smell.

The trio approached Cobra's black muscle car and got in without another word of protest. We were pullin out the deck in a matter of what felt like seconds.

"Race you out the city!" Cobra yelled through his passenger window.

"The fuck? Nooooo!" I yelled at Grimm, drawn out as he hit the throttle and we shot off down the street.

I was terrified for a good two minutes until I slightly relaxed my lethal grip and let myself be in the moment.

The city was so quiet, Cobra had been right. You could hear the engine of the motorcycle and the muscle car crystal clear.

All was well until he began steering with one damn hand and whipped out his scythe like blade with the other.

"What are you doing!?" I yelled over the wind and engine.

"Up on the right," he replied, speaking louder than I'd ever heard him.

I looked over his shoulder, and sure enough, there were two of the men Blue had been talking about, darting towards a rusted out bucket they'd probably stolen from someone else.

Knowing Grimm's intention, I held on a little tighter and braced for impact. He zipped around a huge pothole, right onto the sidewalk.

I was positive he ran over the bones of someone, hearing the loud crunch as they crumbled.

With one hand out, he rode right past the man closest to us, maneuvered around the front of the car, and never slowed down.

I didn't think anything had happened at first, until I felt the fresh blood that had blown back onto my face. Quickly glancing over my shoulder, I saw the man on the ground and his comrade standing over him.

I rubbed my face clean on Grimm's shirt, feeling him laugh.

Aside from that, we almost made it out scot-free. Grimm was moving too fast for the Venom to do much but stare stupidly after us every time he abruptly went down an alley, or evaded them by taking a narrow route they couldn't. A few old people sat on the porches of their houses, enjoyin the show. I reckoned this was the most excitement they'd seen in years around here.

There was only one incident more, and it was quickly handled by Cobra.

A man came spinning out of an alley on his own bike, much too close for comfort. So close that if he wanted to reach out and grab me, he'd probably succeed.

I thought that was his intention, but at the last second, Grimm banked left and Cobra's car came from the right, smashing into the man. He and his bike went in two separate directions.

The red motorcycle screeched and sparked as it spun into an old stoplight on its side. The man might have lived if Cobra hadn't driven right over him as if he was a mere speed bump.

We left Rivermouth behind, and the sun had long set. We were a lil bit closer to being able to end all this and get back home—if it were every truly over.

Chapter Seventeen

Arlen

It wasn't possible to make it in a day.

We rode for what felt like ever, and then stopped, finding a semi clearing in the woods to rest in.

Katya and her friends were still with us. I had no idea what would be done with them come the end, but they were good company.

Cobra had started a fire, tossed down a bag with food in it, and then went off to speak with Grimm, standing where I could see them and they me.

I leaned against a tree, using Grimm's atomic bag as a cushion, munching on hard tacks dipped in peanut butter to add flavor to the bland crackers. I had Grimm's hoodie on so I wasn't cold.

I'd never been campin before, but I reckoned it was similar to this. Blue and Parker were fast asleep on the other side of the fire, using one another as pillows.

"So what's the deal with you and them?" Katya asked from beside me, nodding her head in Grimm's general direction. She had on a jacket I was certain belonged to Cobra, and was still wearin her bloody blue skirt.

I should've warned her she might not want to go that route, but they were both older than me. Who was I to tell either of them what to do?

Her question had a barrage of answers I could have given; I chose to keep it simple, with a Cliff Notes version.

"Grimm is mine, Cobra is my brother, and the woman who started this all isn't with them. She's at home about to have the devil's spawn."

"You mean Calista, right?" she asked, helpin herself to my peanut butter.

I grinned, because that was such a me move.

"I forget how widely known she is. To me, she's just Cali." I sat the peanut butter between us so she could stop stretching over my lap to get it.

My line of vision was cut off by Grimm's return. He wordlessly sat down, and nearly dragged me onto his lap.

"What's the deal with you and them?" I asked her, shiftin to get comfy.

"We kind of just banded together. Blue and I know each other from being in the same city. Parker was a tag-along. We didn't have a destination until now."

"They're coming with us to get Noah." Cobra joined us, answering my silent question.

"Why would you do that?" I asked Katya directly.

"An initiation." She shrugged. "We have nowhere to go, no real protection. Why not join the cult no one wants to mess with?"

"Understandable," I said slowly. I'd understood long ago. What else was there for people to do when being a loner often equaled death? Safety in numbers seemed a logical solution, in my humble opinion. Isn't that why people had banded together inside Centriole?

And who better to join than the gang that dominated the Badlands, just like Katya said? But… "What initiation?"

"Do you remember when you wanted in? We made you come with us to the church and the cannibal farm. They'll be coming with us to wherever we get sent," Cobra answered.

"Oh." I didn't know what else to say. He didn't seem to care if they made it in or not; neither did Grimm.

"Blue and I spontaneously left the city because it sounded better than the norm. We had families and friends try and talk us out of it, but we just wanted to see what was in the great beyond. You see how well that's worked out for us?"

She was making light of their situation, but I obviously knew what it was like to be smacked with reality.

"What city are ya'll from?"

"Prescott, you know, the one with the blue trees?"

I blinked like an idiot, course I didn't know, because Dad said there was no other city aside from The Kingdom.

"If you had all that, why come here?"

"We have rape, murder, thieves, and corruption. The slick streets just pretty it all up."

“This may be hell, but it gives you more freedom than what many consider heaven.”

I didn’t have a response to that, but I heard the sadness in her voice. I had the distinct feelin she’d killed long before the hospital hallway.

We each had our own story to tell.

We all had our own demons, and had the option of making peace with em or vanquishing em in our own way. At the end of the day, it didn’t matter, because we all had to go to sleep and wake up again until we died.

Hopefully, they’d survive long enough to figure it out. Katya and Blue seemed like the type of women you’d want around.

“Come with me, Brat,” Grimm suddenly said, lifting me off him.

He took my hand and led me a little way from our group. Leaning himself against a tree, he pulled me to stand in front of him.

“Just spill it Grimm,” I huffed when it became clear he was hesitatin.

He rolled his shoulders, tightenin his grip on my hand as if he was worried I would bolt.

"Do you remember at the old compound? There was a room full of belongings: clothes, identification cards—."

"A wallet belonging to James Wallace? The missing Centriole Inspector?"

"Exactly like that. I know you're aware of the men being sent outside of the wall," he said.

I nodded slowly, already formin a hunch.

Armed men were often sent out when a power grid needed servicing, or a waterline needed a weld. Very rarely did that whole batch of workers return. How absurd was the notion that the council men would risk their own lives to ensure they had electricity and runnin water? Those gluttonous fuckers didn't even pick their own strawberries.

Honestly, I'd never thought of the two in any relation but now that Grimm brought that specific room up, it was damn impossible not to put the pieces together.

“Keep goin,” I said, feelin a small bubble of apprehension as I waited for him to confirm my theory.

“Your father added in people who he felt opposed something he was doing, or disagreed with him on whatever he wanted to bitch about for the day, ensuring they wouldn’t be going back home.”

“And that’s where Romero comes in,” I finished, answering one of my earlier questions. “But what does he get out of it?”

“What he got was a shitload of food we, clothes, fucking bubble bath….the buyer for Luca’s skin farm.”

I took a step back to process what he was sayin. That my dad had been sendin entire families to their deaths…all to hold a fuckin position? I knew he was a power hungry hypocrite, but he was a murderer, too?

I *knew* the answer, had seen the facts, and it sickened me.

James Wallace had a place on the city council, he disappeared, and one of Dad's idiot friends took his place.

James also had a six month old baby, twins, and a wife—that all mysteriously disappeared. And he wasn't the only one.

When one family left, another took its place. But they weren't leavin on their own free will.

"Grimm, that's…. like fuckin genocide. No wonder the goddamn population never changed." I pulled my hand free and began to pace, wishin that sonofabitch was in front of me right that very moment.

Pausing, I turned back towards Grimm. "What happened to those lil babies? Did you…?" I couldn't even finish that sentence. "I know you've done a lot of sick shit, like the cannibal farm, and I've accepted that but if you've been—."

His mask slipped for a brief second and he looked a combination of pissed and disgusted before it was back in place.

He stood taller, his body tensing with his anger.

“I kill cannibalistic little fuckers beyond the point of being human ever again.

“I don’t kill cherub faced babies because your dad’s a fuckin pussy who had you and everyone behind that wall brainwashed, believing in fucking fairies and bullshit utopias.”

I crossed my arms, glad they were hidden beneath his hoodie. I had fairy tattoos, didn’t take a genius to know that was leveled at me. I opened my mouth to respond but he wasn’t done yet.

“Your dad sent them to the same place he had you and your uncle taken.”

“Me and—what? Why would he do that?”

“How would I know that Arlen? He’s your dad.”

"The same man throwing a tantrum because Romero doesn't need him anymore, same man who paid Noah to keep you locked away and supplied birth control so he could stick his dick in you. And then your ma sent Beth out here to–."

"Now you're just full of shit, Ma would never—."

"Use her own daughters to help further your dad's agenda and then play the victim?"

Ouchie. She damn sure would do somethin like that. They all would. But the truth felt like a barely closed wound bein torn wide open again. I didn't want to sit and think about all the implications right then, I needed a different pain to focus on.

"You interrupt me again and I'm gonna kick your balls into your stomach!" I glared at Grimm.

He through his back and laughed.

Not a little chuckle or a three second I'm-too-cool to show emotion laugh, but a real gut bustin laugh.

I marched towards him, knowing exactly what to do for the reaction I wanted.

My hand was connectin with his face before I had one second to reconsider. The sting on my palm had just registered when he grabbed hold of me by the throat, slightly liftin me off the ground.

"Get…off," I croaked, clawing at his arm.

I heard someone yell in the background, It was Spanish, so I assumed it came from Katya.

Grimm let me go, sweepin my feet out from underneath me in the process. I landed on my ass; he swooped down and flipped me onto my stomach, makin me land face first in a pile of leaves, pushing his weight on my back to keep me down.

I lifted my head and yelled up at him "What the entire hell do you think you're doin?"

"You're a pain in the fucking ass, Brat. If you want to hit like a little kid and throw a tantrum, you can get your ass smacked like a little kid." He tore my pants down, draggin my underwear with em.

"Don't you dare!" My shrill voice echoed across the tree tops.

"Shut the fuck up." He cupped my mouth.

Arousal was already floodin between my. He brought his palm down right on my naked flesh. I yelped, immediately tryna get away. He did it again, and again. I counted twelve hits in, rapid succession.

I was still on the ground, tryna catch my breath, my clit on fire, when I heard his zipper.

He yanked his hoodie off me, letting me drop back down only after he pulled my tits out of my tank top. Grippin my hips, he slammed into my drenched pussy with no pretenses, fuckin me so hard I dug my nails into the ground to try and keep still.

I was so wet I could feel it coatin my thighs, drippin down his dick and onto his balls. “You’re a filthy whore,” he grumbled, fisting my hair, pounding me into the dirt.

“Yes,” I moaned in agreement, my ass still burnin from the heat of his hits.

“You’re my pretty little pain-slut.”

“All yours,” I breathed. He let my hair go and grabbed somethin behind him.

“You could have just asked for it, Brat. You want me to hurt you? That’s all it takes. Apparently you don’t trust me enough to give you what you need or you wouldn’t have pulled that bitch of a stunt. I know you’re hurting, baby. I’ll always make it better.”

I blinked the thick burnin tears away. I needed him to stop talkin and make me feel nothin but us in this moment.

“Doin a shitty job of it. Maybe someone else can do better.”

He laughed, but there was no warmth in it.

I was just thinkin I'd pushed too far, only to slightly relax when nothin happened, which was exactly what he was waitin on.

"Grimm," I whimpered as soon as I felt the coolness of the curved blade against my throat. It was still covered in the blood of its last victim.

My pussy clenched, loving the very idea, but my heart rate jumped to concerning levels.

"Remember that conversation about me being a possessive dick? If you ever say that stupid shit to me again, I'll slit your throat open and shove my cock inside as you choke on your own blood. No one will ever touch you again but me. I have no problems taking out any man who thinks it's an option." He pushed himself so deep inside me, it hurt.

His words made me feel fuckin wonderful, completely owned. I wanted more. The blade threatened to end me, make me bleed out all over the earthy terrain.

I trusted him to cut me just enough to satisfy the painful ache I craved and make it sting. He began thrustin in and out painstakingly slow, makin me take his cock inch, by thick, hard inch.

"You want me to fuck you bloody? Remember you asked for this."

He added pressure to the blade. I moaned as it bit into my skin, the burn increasing the pressure in my lower stomach.

I felt the blood begin to trickle a split second before he pulled the knife away. Immediately, he had the blade pressing into the flesh of my shoulder, diggin in hard enough to make me flinch.

He was quick and efficient with whatever he was doin. In less than ten seconds, he had the blade tossed to the side and was shoving me further into the ground as he lifted my hips.

Cupping some of the blood running down my neck, he leaned back slightly to reposition himself and spread my left cheek open. Using his bloody fingers, he pressed into my ass.

I tensed, my breath catchin in my throat. No one had touched me there since that night.

I remembered the tearing and the pain, suddenly wanting to feel it from him. I knew he'd make it better. He repeated the same process as before, this time taking the sticky crimson from my shoulder.

"Next time, I'll carve the R," he flippantly said.

I didn't understand what he'd meant right away, realizing he'd carved the first letter of his name into my skin a second too late.

He had the head of his cock lined up at the rim, and was shoving the fingers he'd just used to lube me in my mouth.

"You're going to scream. Bite down," he commanded, fully burying himself inside my ass.

It wasn't an option not to do as he said.

My jaw slammed together as he viciously plunged in and out of the sensitive hole. I screamed, feelin my legs tremble. The pain and pleasure had unfettered tears streaming down my face.

He battered me completely. I couldn't take it.

My body was a live wire one minute and a ragin inferno of pure bliss the next. I cried out, the pleasure shredding me apart as I hit a peak I'd never climbed before and hurtled over the edge.

He rode my body for what felt like hours, leavin me a boneless pile of mush by time he climaxed. I was barely aware I was even breathin when he smeared his excess semen and my come into my bloody skin before bringing them back to my mouth. I sucked them clean like they were coated in an elixir.

Suddenly, he grinned and looked over his shoulder. "You enjoy the show you sick fuck?"

Oh, lawd. I pulled my mouth from his fingers and hid my face.

"Personally, Grimmy, I would have added a bit more rhythm, but I'll give you a solid eight out of nine!" Cobra yelled from the other side of the clearing, following it with a laugh.

I shook my head, fighting my own grin. I hadn't even realized the damn peepin Tom was watchin us.

Grimm maneuvered me so I was on my side and he could press himself into my back.

"You're fucking beautiful, Brat," he murmured, running his hand over my hip, both of us fell silent, spent, lying in the dirt.

I didn't care I had leaves all in my hair, my skin was stinging where he'd cut me open, or that I probably wouldn't be able to walk come sunrise.

.I was addicted to the way he numbed the hurt in my brain by givin me a different kind of pain. He made my worn heart ache in the best way possible.

Grimm had never been the cure; he'd always been the disease. My fucked up remedy, a poison I would willingly ingest until my dying day.

"Knowing or not knowing what you do now, do you ever miss your old life?" he asked me, toying with a strand of my hair.

We were still lying on the ground, but clothed again, his hoodie a blanket. I was certain my body was nothin more than a stiff piece of cardboard at the moment.

We'd only been awake maybe thirty minutes, but I was ready to get this conversation over with now.

I looked up at his bearded face. Naturally, I could've just told him no, but it was somewhat of a lie.

I missed my uncle, and I missed Ma even now she'd completely broken my heart, but that was the extent of it.

Right then, I missed razors, and shampoo, showers, hot meals, Cali, and even Romero. I missed the paradise of burning bodies and the surprise of bumping into a man in a black hooded robe and white satanic mask at three in the morning.

I didn't miss the house, pool boy, or that ugly wall. Didn't miss Dad, or even Beth, my half-sister, who I assumed was dead at this point in the game. She'd never done anything but try and hurt me or the family I'd come to love. They may have been Savages, but even wolves had loyalty that coursed through their blood.

"What if I told you I didn't give a damn about my old life, cause that's exactly what it is?

Being here with you, killin our way back to our corner of dark paradise where the devil's awaitin…that's my life now, and I happen to like it much better."

"Oh yeah?" He settled his hands on my hips. "Death doesn't scare you anymore?"

"Oh, it does. But I love it, almost as much as I love you." I smiled and wrapped one arm round the back of his neck, bringing us closer together. I didn't expect him to say it back, didn't even care if he thought I was psycho for sayin those three little words so soon.

I'd been crazy about him far too long to give a damn. I could wait on him to love me back.

"That's irony at its finest, because I think you're the only thing I've ever been scared shitless of in my life," he said, his gravelly voice so soft it almost sounded like he'd whispered.

My lips parted, but only air came out. If I made a big deal of his brutally honest confession, he would shut down.

I knew what he was tellin me, and no words would replace the actions that needed to be taken.

I was scared of lovin him, and it uncharted territory for both of us. We didn't trust the normalcy and feared the solid foundation. The thing with love was that you couldn't touch it, couldn't hold onto it and be sure it would never change.

I took a shaky breath, cupped his strong jaw, and opened my wound a little more, letting him in deeper. That was going to be my strategy until he found a home inside me.

"The mayor of Centriole isn't my real dad. My uncle and my mom had an affair. I didn't find out until I was nine and overheard an argument. I was raised away from him, but he knew the truth. We were…close. He let me be myself.

"I've always been a black sheep, an outcast in my own home."

"I think I know why the man who raised me set me up to die. I'm an original family disappoint. He never really wanted me in the first place, he just didn't want to be publicly humiliated by ma." I laughed, but damn did the truth hurt to the ninth degree of hell. I'd never caused anyone harm back then.

I felt like I'd been pushed into becoming this version of myself. I'd been done a huge favor. Grimm cupped my face, makin me give him my eyes, peerin right down to my brittle core. He didn't care that I was bitter.

He didn't care I was full of hate. He looked at me as if I was golden, every single time.

"When you break from the flock to be an individual instead of a mindless sheep, you're suddenly something foreign, a freak."

"The woman who raised me after I got out of The Order…she didn't like me very much either, she made that clear to me and my father. She left when I was nine, haven't seen her since."

I took his hand and threaded my fingers with his. "Fuck those people."

"That's been my motto a lot longer than it's been yours, Brat."

I lightly nudged his shoulder, managing a small smile through my tears.

Chapter Eighteen

Arlen

We left at sunrise and arrived at sunset.

Plymouth was much more of a town than a– city– but it was full of vitality. Just like Rivermouth, the welcome sign was a tribute to Romero, but this sigil had *memento mori* scrawled across the ram's head.

People were walkin outside looking completely unbothered. There was a rundown diner with raw pink, freshly butchered pigs hangin in the window. Kids tossed a ball back and forth in an empty field.

The houses I was able to see were like lil cabins, cute and tidy. The majority of them had some type of sugar skull, leviathan cross, or ram head décor in their yards or windows.

A church with a giant inverted cross in the middle of a fire pit looked like the most cared for building around.

Clearly, this town took their worshippin to an extremely disturbing level. Anyone who saw Grimm or Cobra stopped what they were doin and waved or yelled out *ave Satanás*, like they were rootin for a damn sports team. Sometimes it was truly disconcerting how deep this all went.

Lucy's sat at the very edge, and I wasn't sure what to expect, but this…wasn't it.

The sign was a giant piece of white wood with the name written in bold blue font, stamped with a small leviathan cross in the corner. The actual building looked like a mini apartment building in major need of some siding.

A large dictation of the Sigil of Baphomet was painted on the side in red with the same *memento mori* scrawled across it. Dark curtains prohibited anyone from seeing a peep inside.

There was no sign of the acolytes, so I was assumin they hadn't arrived yet. Grimm cut the bike's engine in a parking spot beside a decent lookin sedan. A second later, Cobra's Charger pulled up beside us.

Katya smiled and waved at me from the passenger seat and I returned the gesture, lookin away when I heard a door open.

A man with salt n pepper hair stepped out adjustin his belt buckle, and pecked a familiar lookin redhead on the cheek. A huge smile spread across her face when she saw us, gesturing for us to come in.

When she turned back around, I saw the inverted cross on her left shoulder where her silken robe had slipped down.

"Grimm, where exactly are we?" I asked, hissin slightly as he lifted me off his bike and my body reminded me it was in dire need of some real rehabilitatin. Thankfully, he had the hindsight to keep a tight grip on me, because I felt like I was standin in quick sand.

"It's a place fine upstanding men like myself sometimes come to receive pleasure, and then we go on our way," Cobra answered, climbin out of his car. "You're lookin sore, sis," he smirked, laughing when I flipped him off.

"You brought us to a whore house?" Katya asked, joining the conversation.

"Kat, they're called brothels now," Blue laughed, sidling up to Cobra.

I quirked a brow at him, knowin full well he'd just been cozy with Katya the day prior.

She seemed unbothered by it, goin as far as smiling at the two of em together. Parker curiously studied Lucy's, keepin whatever he was thinkin to himself.

Cobra instantly lost his playful appeal.

Was it only obvious to me he was trying to make Kat jealous? With a soft sigh, I turned back to Grimm, who was undoing the bag from his bike.

“Why are we at a brothel?”

“Because it’s where Rome told us to be, where our lead is, so we can go end this, get home and start working on the next generation.” He looped the bag of his shoulder and then headed for the building, leavin me to follow.

What the did he mean? I hoped to high hell it wasn’t a damn baby.

“Damn *cabrona*, I would love to find a man who bossed me like that. I’ve yet to meet one with balls bigger than mine.” Kat looped her arm in mine and urged me forward, payin no mind to the look on Cobra’s face.

I had to swallow a retort, refusin to get in between whatever they had goin on. I heard an old Creed song blastin through a stereo system as we drew closer.

Grimm stepped right inside, leaving the music to pour out as we followed him in.

The room smelled of cigarette smoke and potpourri. It had been converted. If/when illicit activities happened, it was clearly very private. There was a large bar in the back left corner where two men sat nursing drinks.

A few more were playin a game of cards.

Women sat around seemingly content, dressed in comfortable lookin lingerie. A Baphomet banner like the one Cali had in her bedroom hung on a wall.

"Grimm, Cobra, bout time ya'll showed your faces around here. How long has it been? Six months, almost?" the redhead asked as she approached with a genial smile on her pretty face.

I side eyed Grimm but his expression gave nothin away. "Rome told you we were coming?" he asked, getting right to the point.

"Yeah." Her smiled slipped a bit.

"Your regular rooms are ready, and room four's been prepped for your friends. No one will bother you. Romero's message is with Tucker." She gestured to the bartender.

"Come on, Brat," he said over his shoulder, pushing past her and headin towards the wooden stairs. We went up, going to the door with a golden number two on it. He pushed it open and gestured for me to enter before him.

"Meet me down at the bar in five," he said to Cobra, who had stopped at a door across the hall.

My assumption about this being an apartment building was correct. I stood in the efficiency and looked around. There was a cornflower blue sofa pulled out into a neatly made queen sized bed with a wicker basket atop it. There was a simple kitchenette, a full sized bathroom through another door, and had simple light gray painted on the walls. It was clean and cozy-ish.

Approachin the bed, I looked at the contents loaded in the basket and could have wept. Body wash, shampoo, a two pack of women's razors. There was a toothbrush, the holy grail of hygiene products. No one wanted their breath smellin like pork loin.

"I'm going to give you and the basket a few minutes alone." Grimm half-joked.

"The shower works; just give it a minute. There's a platter in the fridge to eat for now and the bed is fresh. We won't be here long, but I want you to sleep a little because you know what happens next."

"Do *you* ever miss your old life?" I found myself repeating his own question back to him before he could go anywhere. I was genuinely curious.

I waved my hand around the room, "We're standin in a town that worships you, in an old fuck pad you were at months ago, so… don't go gettin the big headed notion I'm jealous, I am, but not cause you were with other people.

"That's to be expected we weren't together, and you got to get your kicks from somewhere," I quickly explained.

He palmed his hair back, shaking his head with a slight twitch of his mouth. "The only thing different about my life is that I have you in it. What's there to miss?

"I don't miss fucking the mannequins' who lie there and moan like I've stuck a Jesus piece inside them. I know my dick's pretty fucking amazing, but that doesn't do anything for me, just like they never did. They were irrelevant, Brat. Sure as fuck don't have shit on you."

"That was real sweet, but you could've stopped at the whole, *I am your entire life and you need me portion,*" I softly joked. "You can go do whatever you gotta do. Imma get acquainted with your shower. But…I'm sorry for what I said. Well, mostly all of it, actually. I wouldn't really go mess with another man, that wasn't very nice." I was rather proud of myself for that spiel.

Holding my hands clasped together, I waited for him to say somethin.

"Come a little closer. Let me tell you a secret."

Squinting my eyes, I slowly inched towards him, stopping when we were nearly chest to chest.

"I already knew that, Brat." He gripped my jaw, adding a bit of pressure, leaning down so his mouth was skimming mine. "No one's gonna touch you the way I touch you, see you the way I see you, break you down, use you, and then build you up like I do. You're not going anywhere. You're mine."

He kissed me, sealin his proclamation roughly, giving it back twice as hard when I reciprocated, nippin my lower lip and soothing the split skin with his skilled tongue before he finally let go.

He was out the door without another word, leavin me alone to clean every crevice on my body and some time to think.

I grabbed the basket and went into the bathroom, seeing a stack of plush towels on a rack.

Pulling the plastic shower liner to the side, I spun the brass nozzle nearly as far it would go, and then waited. Pipes groaned and it sounded like footsteps running inside the wall, but eventually the spicket shook and water began spraying out.

I wasn't goin to bother lookin in the mirror till I was finished; no need to see what the hell Grimm had been looking at the last few days. I may have been an emotional, unstable, occasionally badass lil bitch, but I was still a lady.

I slowly peeled off my clothes, definitely feelin everything Grimm had done to me. There were dark bruises between my thighs, and the scabby skin where he'd cut me flexed with my every movement.

My ass would never be the same again, of that I was certain, and he'd buried himself inside it for what seemed like a good hour.

Going to the bathroom was not on my top five things to do list, but I did need to pee.

That hurt, too.

Yeah, this was gonna be a pain.

But so worth it. Thirty minutes, maybe hours later—who knows? my scalp was clean, my fur was gone, and my muscles had some much needed relief. I hadn't been in a real shower in so long, I could've stayed there for months.

Sinking down in the porcelain tub, I let the spray come down on me and shut my eyes for a minute. Everythin I'd learned should have dramatically impacted me, but I didn't really feel any more hurt than I already had—with the exception of Ma.

Not even *her* actions surprised me as much as they voided the last bit of love I had for her.

People would do anything to hold onto a semblance of power. The mayor was no different; he was just the shittiest kind of person, because he hid behind smoke and mirrors.

It didn't seem right to think of him as my dad at this point, when he had never really been such a thing. I'd had tutors and nannies, never real parents. My ma gave that up to join him in his quest to rule a city.

My real father was good to me, but we weren't permitted to spend countless hours together. He'd died in the worst way possible, but I refused to dredge up that initial feelin of loss. I'd numbed myself to it from the moment his life left his body.

This all seemed to have happened so long ago that when I thought of it, it was like seeing it from stranger's perspective. It only made me wonder: why now? Why was the mayor going through such lengths to find me?

Why was he having Noah keep me locked away? What purpose did it hold? Knowin Ma and Beth were in on it only added fuel to my fire and a deeper sense of urgency to figure out what the hell was goin on.

When the water began runnin cold, I made myself climb out of the shower, wrappin a towel around my body after wringing out my hair.

Brushing my teeth, I let myself see my reflection.

Nothing had changed. I still looked the same. Switchin off my moral compass hadn't made me look any different on the outside. But *everything* was different.

I had a past and a present. Like I'd told Grimm, it was a past I wanted to leave behind. I was ready to end this and go home. I was ready to move on and live again.

I stared in the mirror and found a genial smile liftin the corners of my mouth.

The faint red line on my throat was a reminder he'd had the curve of his blade against it less than twenty-four hours ago. Turning, I laughed, shakin my head when I saw the perfect inverted cross beside a G embellished in my flesh.

Chapter Nineteen

Grimm

Our lead came written on a napkin.

Tucker, the bartender, had it wrapped around the V tattoo of the neck of whomever he'd got the information from.

"Forkfurt Penitentiary?" Cobra read from beside me, chugging down a shot. "How the fuck is anyone living in that place? It's falling apart."

I waved for Tucker to come over when he was finished with his conversation. I felt a heavy pair of tits pressing into my left arm as I lowered the right.

I knew who it was; I'd seen her watching me from the second we arrived. I wasn't going to give her any of the attention she was seeking.

Being so brazenly touched didn't sit right with me, never had, unless it was Brat.

I couldn't keep my hands off her, couldn't *not* touch her.

Without glancing over, I shoved the bitch attached to the tits away from me. I heard her teeter on her heels, and then fall, landing on her ass with an outraged gasp, making Cobra laugh. I still didn't look over, that would mean I gave a fuck.

"With you and Rome being locked down I feel a little left out. Don't suppose you wanna do the whole ménage thing?" Cobra asked.

Had he been anyone else I would have reached over and broken his spine vertebra by vertebra, and then I'd probably piss on him just for the hell of it.

"She's…"

"Don't hurt your precious brain trying to explain. She's the reason we're here right now, why were about to go invade a prison. I get it, bro. Rome was, is, the same way. I was joking, fucking psycho," he laughed, holding his hands up in a defensive gesture.

"Isn't that what you've got with Katya? That is why you chose to initiate her, right? Because we both know the mute with the dreads won't be around much longer, and Blue is fifty-fifty."

"No. Katya is a cool-ass chick. And I like Blue, she's my friend. I *am* capable of being just friends with a chick Grimmy."

I scoffed in the back of my throat.

"Since when? You only stayed clear of Cali because you knew what would happen otherwise. You won't touch Brat, because, well, you know what would happen otherwise." I let it go at that, holding back the rest of what I wanted to say until a better time.

"You'll find someone," I felt the need to add. And I meant it.

He was the nicest out of all of us. He openly laughed, had a non-stop sense of humor, and at the end of the day, when push came to shove, you wanted him on your side.

We'd all been through shit. We were all tediously fringing on a blurred line of insanity. Cobra was more fucked in the head than I was, and Romero was so fucked up he had no semblance of empathy until Cali.

This world wasn't what went to utter shit; the people had. I admittedly had it the easiest, if you could discount the fact I was raised by my now estranged father, a reformed cult member, the current leader of a redneck tribe of cannibals, I could almost be considered normal.

The death shit didn't count. Death was nothing but an appointment that couldn't be cancelled. It was a natural part of life that too many saw as unnatural.

In death, life still meant what it always had. The definition didn't suddenly change. Death was nothing but an inescapable fate. We were all going to be ash and bone in the end, I just happened to hand out the ultimatums.

One day, I'd be like everyone else, nothing but a rotting corpse. I was a demon, a nightmare that would eventually meet a tragic end. It was inevitable.

But that wasn't fucking today.

Until now I hadn't gave much thought about the years beyond. Now, I had someone to offer the world to.

She was willing to reign over the dead right beside me. By time we sank into the ground, they'd whisper fables about us.

Having what I needed from Tucker, I headed for the stairs, telling Cobra we were leaving as soon as the acolytes arrived and to meet me upstairs in ten minutes.

I didn't want Brat in this fucking place, but it made the most sense for a rendezvous point. This was our town, specifically for me.

Cobra had one a few miles east. Romero had done it so we always had places to regroup if need be. Usually, it was the three of us. Shit had certainly changed.

Using my key, I unlocked the room door and stepped inside.

She was lying on the bed wrapped in a towel. Her hair was fanned out around her head, long lashes closed over her eyes.

How the fuck could anyone want to change her? How could I ever doubt what she'd become? Any version of her was beautiful. She was a goddess, a masterpiece. Fuck anyone who'd never seen it.

I walked to the bed, reached down, and ran my finger over the line on her neck. Her eyes flew open, and the second she saw me, she smiled, showing a mouthful of pearls.

"When do we leave?" she asked, bouncing up like a cork screw.

"Calm down, killer." I chuckled at her enthusiasm.

She launched herself at me, unashamedly letting her towel fall away as she wrapped her arms around my neck.

"Brat, I was gone less than an hour."

"Shut up and let me cling."

I kissed the side of her face and she leaned into it like she always did, starving for affection. As her man, it was my job to make her never want for a damn thing—starting with that, which reminded me of something I shouldn't have said.

"Why fairies?" I asked her, tracing the one on her arm.

"I like the idea of things that have the freedom to fly away."

"Because you couldn't."

She nodded, touching the one a little lower. "This is my winged succubus; I only got it because she looked badass."

She lifted her shoulder where a dragon was wrapped around the symmetrical black and white circle that represented yin and yang.

"Guessin you know all about this one."

Then, she held up her wrist. "My henna owl, cause she's majestic, wise, and rare."

"Like you," I said, leaning in and trailing kisses down her neck. She smelled like fucking peaches.

"I'm not fuckin wise, Grimm," she laughed.

"But you're majestic and rare?" I moved to her chest.

"Well, kinda." She shrugged. "Now tell me somethin about you. And make it good." I heard the slight change in her breath, felt her pulse jump. Her hands settled on my shoulders as I moved lower, kissing and suckling on her golden skin.

"I belong to you."

"I already knew that."

"Did you know I belonged to you from the very beginning, before I even knew I did?"

"Aw, Grimm."

"And this." I sat her on the edge of the bed, lifting her soft thighs over my shoulders, before placing a hand on her navel to make sure she couldn't go anywhere.

Right over the largest fucking fairy tat she had. “This is my favorite tattoo, because the wings lead straight to your pussy.”

I had my mouth on her clit and my tongue working up and down her slit before she could reply.

It didn’t take her long to thread her dainty fingers through my hair. I looked up, eyes traveling over the sinewy curves of her tiny body, and grinned. “Roll your hips, fuck my tongue, and don’t stop until you’re coming in my mouth.”

That was all the directive she needed. She pulled herself closer, using my hair as leverage, and shoved me nose deep inside her.

I happily, greedily sucked and ate her like I was at my last meal, and she was the entrée.

Her pussy tasted like pomegranates, and her melodic moans were the key to Pandora ’s Box. Fuck, this girl was all my favorite sins in one imperfect vessel.

When the door clicked shut, I knew she heard it, but she didn't stop me, In fact, she pulled me even deeper.

I was acutely aware of Cobra's presence, never pausing in my ministrations. I heard him take a seat in the old wooden table chair after he dragged it a little closer.

I'd seen the way he watched her the night before. I remembered the flair of excitement in her eyes in the parking deck at the thought of an audience.

This was a onetime thing.

I'd usually pass who I was with right over to him if we weren't smashing her between us.

But he couldn't touch her; I'd take his hand off before that happened, and I knew she wouldn't let him.

When I heard him undoing his pants, I knew it was good enough, regardless.

Brat's legs began to tighten around my head, her movements not as sporadic.

She moaned my name and I almost came my damn self. I could hear Cobra roughly fisting his dick where he sat, knew he was hard from the full visual in front of him.

I nipped at her clit, digging my fingers into her thighs where I knew she was the sorest.

I growled when she roughly tugged on my strands in response. Her arousal was dripping down onto my beard. I was swimming between her thighs.

My hair felt like it was about to detach right with my scalp, Brat didn't give a fuck. She only cared about coming all over my taste buds.

I bit down on her swollen nub and made it happen. Her hips would have lifted clean off the bed if I wasn't holding her down.

I undid my pants, flicking her clit back and forth with the tip of my tongue, triggering another spasm from her body. I had her pinned by the throat, legs still over my shoulders, dick hard and pushing inside her with no warning.

As soon as she was lucid enough, she grabbed for me, urging me to tear her ass up like she knew I would. I fucked her like a whore every single time. She loved this shit as much as I did. Fucking each other up in bed had become our thing.

I looked at her pussy and swore I saw my reflection staring back at me. She was so wet I felt like I needed to dick her down a little harder to ensure she felt every inch of me branding inside her. Her face contorted, frozen in an overwhelming state of pleasure.

"Damn, this is intense," I heard Cobra groan, Brat's pussy clenched in response. I'd almost forgotten he was even in the room.

I switched positions, spreading Brat as wide as I could, sitting back on my hunches so Cobra had a better visual of my dick moving in and out of her tight, saturated pussy.

"Make her scream," he soughed, cupping his balls in one hand and stroking himself with the other.

Brat angled her hips, allowing me to bottom out. She shut her eyes and bit down on her bottom lip trying to muffle her moans.

"Open your eyes, Brat, don't fight it. Let me hear how good my dick feels." I grabbed her tits, firmly, and squeezed, kneading the shit out of them.

Hey eyes flew open same time as her mouth, giving me and Cobra what we both wanted.

He groaned again, the sound had my own balls lifting and brat digging her nails into my wrists, pleading with her sexy ass eyes she wanted to come. I pulled one hand away and slapped her clit, rubbing the sting away with my fingers.

"Don't stop," she moaned, locking her legs behind my ass.

I slapped her clit again, forcefully powering pounding into her as her pussy locked down like a vice, come covering my length.

"Goddamn," I heard Cobra huff as he busted his nut, barely audible beneath Brat's screams of pleasure.

It wasn't until I was on my back, so sweaty I was sticking to the sheets, savoring the taste of Brat's pussy that I realized he was gone.

She lay on top of me, her trembling frame fitting perfectly with mine.

"My real name is Gerald," I randomly told her, my voice a little gravellier than usual.

"Gerald is a stupid fuckin name," she laughed, still out of breath.

I lightly slapped her ass and smirked. It was a stupid fucking name.

Chapter Twenty

Arlen

Cobra came bargin into the room just as I finished scrambling to button my shorts.

I could smell the smoke outside the windows from the fires being started around the town. The call of carrion birds and people shoutin is what had awakened me, though.

“How the hell did they find us again?” I asked, hearin another scream from down below.

“Well, Dreads, is missing, so I think that’s our answer.

"Where the fuck's Grimm?" I finished lacing my boot, tossed my hair up in a ponytail, and followed Cobra out into the hall.

He'd been snuggled up right behind me, freshly showered when I dozed again.

I had lots of questions about, Parker, who'd suddenly been demoted to, 'Dreads,' but I figured getting out of the building was a better option to start with.

Katya and Blue were at the top of the stairs. Kat looked ready to kick ass, whereas Blue looked like she was about to have a full blown heart attack.

I made sure she stayed behind us as we descended. The first thing I saw was an acolyte shoving a damn sword through the lower groin of a Venom fucker.

"They arrived right before the last group did," Cobra explained, helpin me off the last stair. I smiled when his silver eyes searched my face, assuring him all was peachy between us after the earlier event.

I liked having another man watch Grimm have his way with me, I didn't know the logistics, but it made me feel good.

The redhead who had greeted us was cowering behind the bar, the bartender lying dead beside her, his throat making a perfect, gaping O.

Another one of the girl's was flat on her back beside the card table, the whole back portion of her head missing. The exposed brain matter looked like raw hamburger meat.

Aside from those minor casualties, the other three bodies belonged to men with the V tattoo. Six acolytes stood around the room like lethal sentries, all in their signature long black robes and white masks with the inverted cross. These satanic fuckers were really startin to grow on me.

"Let's go. They got him at the church." Grimm's voice boomed as he came in the front door.

"I'm driving," he directed at Cobra, coming to grab my hand.

I obediently followed him outside. The smoke smell was ten times worse and the fluttering of wings was hidden behind dark clouds.

There was lots of shoutin and the devil's church lit up like a beacon in the distance.

"Why aren't we goin on the bike?" I asked Grimm, climbin into passenger seat of Cobra's Charger after he pulled the door open for me.

I slid all the way over so Cobra could get in beside me, takin position in the middle. Blue and Katya got in back.

"The only thing they could do that wouldn't attract too much attention— mutilated my tires," he responded as soon as he was in the driver's seat.

"We didn't know," Kat said.

"No shit, you were just the dumbasses he used as a cover," Grimm replied, flying down the road.

I nudged him with a scowl. It wasn't her fault Parker was a shit person.

"If I find out you *were* trying to take my girl away, I'll find everyone you love and slaughter them right in front of you."

He braced a forearm across my chest, and hit the brakes.

If it wasn't for that and Cobra grippin my shoulder I would have flown through the windshield.

"Grimm—."

"And what's happening to them will be child's play compared to what I'll do to you." He cut me off and pointed at the church, indicating the cause of the smoke.

The iron Leviathan cross was glowing a bold orange. Tied to the front of it was Parker, the back held a man who was already too melted to be identifiable. Embers carried pieces of them on the air.

Parker's flesh was already splittin open, and somethin that looked like chunky blocks of thick cheddar was leaking out of him.

That was more disturbin and vile to me than him not being dead and the townies cheering the fire on. His voice was vastly fadin but his screams were audible nonetheless.

The substance leaked onto his clothes, and like a wick, his shirt fed the clumps to the hungry flames, fueling the fire.

It had just begun to consume him entirely as Grimm gunned the engine. I don't think any of us really had anything to say at the moment.

The acolytes followed us in a large SUV.

"We go through the valley and wrap around, surprise em from the back."

"That's smart," Cobra replied.

I looked from side to side, waitin on an explanation. "Are you gonna tell me where we're goin?"

"To cut the head off the snake."

We hit the Valley one bathroom break later, just as the sun came back again.

Grimm pulled the Charger to the side and cut the engine. Once he was out, he held out his hand and slid me towards him.

"It's best to travel light. The sun can be more of a pain in the ass than you are once we go in." He gestured to the tall rocks making up the walls.

"What sun? There's barely anything but darkness in there," Katya said, coming to stand beside me. She'd changed into an outfit much like mine, shorts and a tank top, but still had a large glitter bow attached to her ponytail.

She was right. It looked like the valley of death, irony at its finest.

"You want to go through there? It's the valley of shadows."

"There's not shit to be afraid of. The valley is mine, and the shadows are my bitches."

I closed my eyes, shakin my head as Cobra laughed and held out his hand for a fist bump.

"I bet that made ya feel real badass, didn't it?" I asked.

"Brat, we both already know I'm badass." He took my hand and began leading me forward.

Three acolytes from Lucy's followed closely behind us. The other three were circling around in their SUV.

Cobra fell into conversation with Kat and Blue. By their responses and lack of remorse over Parker, I knew Grimm's first assumption was correct, he'd been using them.

I truly hoped the two of them made it all the way through this.

They were outcasts—just like I was not that long ago. We were all lookin for somewhere we belonged.

This hell was easier to survive with family who willingly went through the worst of days right along with you.

Or in my case, you had a man by your side who opened your eyes a bit to how beautiful it could be. Even the valley with its dark shadows, pinkish walls of rock, and odd lil critters occasionally peeking out at us held a quality of natural beauty.

I glanced over at Grimm and saw he had what looked like a smirk on his face.

"Why are you in such a good mood?" I asked. I couldn't help but smile at em. He was so damn gorgeous.

"Why wouldn't I be? I'm going to do what I do best, and after that's done, I get to take you home."

"Yeah, about that next generation thing…were you talkin about kids?"

He was quiet so long, I began wondering if I'd shoved him back in his bubble.

"I know you're only nineteen, but I'm damn near thirty-years old, Brat. If not now, when?"

"I don't care about your age, Grimm."

"I wouldn't give a shit if you did."

"I love it when you get possessive," I smirked. "Is this coming from you getting to play daddy in the woods the other day?"

"No, but I look forward to daddying the fuck out of you whenever you get out of line."

For real? He was going to owe me a wet floor sign he kept this up.

The thought of havin my reaper's babies one day was enough to make my ovaries implode. Hell, any woman would sign up for that job just to experience the epic ride his cock was. And his wicked tongue.

Still, this was pretty damn huge.

"Shouldn't we figure out our future first?"

"Already know what I'll be doing six years from today, and so do you, because your ass will be right beside me with a big stone on your finger."

"I…will? *You* believe in?" I asked with a quirked brow.

"Our vows will be made before our friends, the forces of darkness, and all the gods of the pit, at the church of Satan."

Ooookay.I waited for a punch line. I should have known that as Grimm had told a joke a total of maybe five times, that was the truth drenched in dark humor.

I almost tripped over my own two feet when I realized he was as serious as he could be. Holy hell, I could see the virginal sacrifices now. He took his Satanism way too seriously for me to say that joke aloud.

As if he'd heard it. Cobra laughed under his breath. "You'll see it all go down when Cali marries Rome." He nudged me with a canteen of water, and I gladly accepted.

I wondered how much longer we'd be walkin.

"Do you need me to say those three little words, Brat?"

"Nope," I answered honestly. At least, not right then I didn't. I would be patient, but I would want them eventually.

"You'd really marry me?" I asked.

He shrugged like that was an answer.

"You'll be mercy. I'll be death."

"You be my Jack, and I'll be your Sally," I quipped in response.

I wasn't sure if he knew what I was referring to but his soft laughter told me he did.

Our conversation ended as he pointed to an opening in the Valley wall a few feet ahead of us.

Apparently, we'd reached our destination.

Chapter Twenty-One

Arlen

It looked like a haunted fortress of crumbling cellblocks and empty guard-towers.

"Well, you definitely picked the right time of day," I mused.

Grass nearly as tall as me surrounded the decaying brick building. The acolytes fanned out so fast I couldn't even see them anymore. They were like mice: mute, sneaky, and fast.

Carrion birds gathered on the roof of the prison. They seemed to be everywhere we went.

Grimm pulled the hood up on his newly acquired black ensemble, his eyes getting that calculated, deadly look in them he wore so well.

Katya surprised me by adjusting a stiletto knife in her boot.

“Will they have guns?” Blue asked.

“Yes, but they won’t pull the trigger unless it’s a last resort. They don’t know the structure of this building, and they’ll realize soon enough we didn’t come alone,” Cobra answered her.

“There’s ten of us—.”

“Much more than that. Romero wouldn’t send us anywhere without ensuring we were ten times stronger than whatever the fuck we’re up against. “In this case, there are twelve people—that’s including Noah, and we all know he can’t fight his way out of shit.”

I could only assume he’d gotten all this information during one of his many vanishing acts for him to be so specific.

We approached the building and my nerves zinged. They all looked ready to fuck shit up, except Blue. She actually looked Blue.

Katya was definitely the backbone of their duo. She seemed shy, reserved, and sweet.

I had a gut feelin she would be the first and only one of us to go. For the first time in awhile, I felt guilty.

"Blue, you stay with us. Cobra, take Kat. I'll meet you in the west wing."

"Go kill some shit, sis," Cobra grinned, droppin a kiss on my cheek before all but dragging Kat away.

"Be safe," I mouthed to her, catchin a small thumb up before I couldn't see her anymore.

"Take this," Grimm said, nudging me with a familiar black gun.

"You actually got it back?" I tucked the solid piece of metal in the waistband of my shorts.

"Cobra did."

Ugh, no further information needed.

"Wait, what about you? What are you gonna use?" I stopped walking and turned towards him.

"I have everything I need. I was going to make you stay behind me, Knew your ass wouldn't listen. Also what you need, because I need it too. I promised to make sure you got what you wanted."

"Regardless, no one is going to fucking touch you. We need Noah and Vance alive but, kill whoever else moves. Just try not to get trigger happy, because foundation, and don't shoot our own people." He smirked at the last part, knowin my aim was pure shit.

"And you stay close to her," he ordered Blue, suddenly serious.

"Stay close, got it. I don't need to hear that twice." She nodded.

How was I ever gonna thank him for any of this?

He'd turned his whole world upside down for me. He was getting ready to massacre in my name. What notion could be sweeter than that?

"Thank you is a real dismal way of—."

"Brat we've been through this, you—."

"Shut up and listen Grimm. Damn."

"If my dad wasn't hellbent on getting me back, your friends from the brothel would still be alive, your towns wouldn't be being invaded, and——." He gripped the back of my neck and brought me flush against him, forcing his tongue in my mouth to shut me up.

Blue shifted uncomfortably in my peripheral.

Grimm pulled away and looked down at me. "You wouldn't have been taken by Noah for some bullshit reason that never existed; I wouldn't have come to find you. We'd still be eyeing each other from across the room, neither of us making a move. You know I'd take you anyway I could get you.

He let me go and stepped away, his face shrouded by his hood. “You ready ?” he asked, holdin out a gloved hand.

I looked at the old prison as the first scream of pain tore through the air. My heart was pounding like I’d just approached a twelve foot drop, ready as hell for me to go over the edge.

I couldn’t say me and this new Arlen were well acquainted yet, but we understood one another just fine. My petals had wilted and thorns took their place. The demon in my head was wide awake, and the venom in my veins churned a thirst for carnage I couldn’t wait to satisfy.

I was a plague none were prepared for. I’d never felt stronger, and with Grimm forever lurking in the shadows, watching over me, I felt damn near invincible. To touch me was to touch death, and death always won.

“I’m ready,” I said, lookin back at Grimm, with a bright smile, and taking his hand.

Just like the hospital, sound echoed.

People's yells of surprise, footsteps, and one single gunshot so far.

Grimm had seemingly vanished, but I knew he was close, I could feel him, and was proven correct when a body seemed to come from nowhere. Blue and I had been on our way up an old staircase when the man came tumbling down.

His head hit the solid metal railing, leaving a ringing crack and blood behind as he free fell to the level below, landing at an obtuse angle with a nasty soundin splat.

I wondered what it said about my relationship when I knew it was my man who killed someone simply by the way they were executed. Clearly, we were very compatible.

"That's eleven," Blue whispered.

We wound up in a long hall lined with cells. I heard a muffled sound comin from the end like a woman was in pain.

Blue and I slowly edged towards it.

There was a ton of dark spots inside the building, but the vaulted skylights that had been installed when the prison was built made it easy enough to see.

The sound was comin from a cell half-way to the end. I had the pretty lil dagger Grimm had given me in hand and was ready to cut shit. The weight of the gun reminded me it was there too, but that was my last resort.

As we closed in, I realized it wasn't pain I was hearin.

Blue made a sound of disbelief, shaking her head. Two people were fuckin in the midst of all this. I reckoned they didn't know what was goin on for that same reason.

I debated for a millisecond if I should let the chick live, but nah. Fuck all of that; I was takin no prisoners.

They didn't see me, until it was too late.

By the time the man realized I'd entered the small cell and gotten the full view of his freckled ass, there was nothin he could do.

I went in full force.

I was on his back with my blade slicin into his throat, making him bottom bitch. He tried to fight back for half a second, the blade sliced deeper, right through arteries, tissue, and muscle. His cock was still nestled between the woman's legs he'd been screwin, and as his body jerked I wondered if this would be considered necrophilia on her end.

Seein as they were on a dingy old cot, we didn't all fit nice and comfortably together.

The man was making weird noises as he bled out. I shoved his head full of brown hair out of my way, and covered the woman's mouth, mufflin her scream as blood sprayed us but, mostly all over her pretty blonde hair—shame.

"Someone's coming," Blue whispered, surprising the hell out of me by doing a similar move Katya had done.

She took over mufflin the blonde's screams by yanking the dirty pillow out from beneath her head and slamming it over her face.

Jumping up, I rolled the man onto the floor as fast, and quietly as I could, then straddled the blonde. She fought like hell to free her face, Blue was stronger than she was though and my bloody knife goin through the bottom of her jaw solved our problem real quick.

The air she expelled was forced right into the crimson pillow. Blue jumped right over her, grabbed me, and pulled me behind the old rusty door just as another Venom entered.

Hawke.

I reacted instinctively.

He spun around to yell and saw me. There was only brief look of surprise that reflected on his face as my boot landed squarely in the center of his stomach.

He went backward, trippin over the body, and goin down. When he attempted to bounce back up he slipped in the blood of his friend.

It covered his shirt, arms, and jeans. I clenched my white-turned-red dagger between my teeth, knowing I would need both hands, and charged.

"Wait," was all he got out.

I managed to hit him hard enough that his head smacked against the stone floor when he fell back again. I straddled him, but because I was just as slippery as he was, I couldn't get the grip or angle I needed on the dagger due to his struggling.

I wrapped both my hands around his damn throat and squeezed. I squeezed with everything in me, digging my nails into his skin and feeling my muscles burn.

I blocked the veins responsible for the oxygen flowing to his brain, knowing it would start to swell as he suffocated.

I watched the color drain from his face and the calipers burst beneath, the skin, making it look like he was bleeding from the inside out.

I waited as his blood pressure plummeted, his heart struggled to beat, and his lungs seared with the burnin sensation I knew all too well when they were deprived of air.

I watched the life leave his body, and mine felt elated. He dropped down with a quiet thump. I simply stared at him. After a second I spat in his face and stood up with Blue's assistance.

"He got off easy," she mumbled, clearly picking up on my body language. I briefly wondered if that was from personal experience, but we didn't have time for conversation.

"Come on," I said, removing the bloody knife from between my teeth. I rolled my lips together to rid them of the taste.

We left the room behind, heading down the remainder of the hall. The prison seemed oddly quiet, all a sudden.

I knew he was behind me without havin to turn around.

"Damn, Brat, you did good." His hands settled on my hips, and he spun me to face him, a full smile waitin to grace me. I swooned inside.

"You saw em?"

"My favorite part was when you choked him out. I might let you try that next time you ride my dick." His smile shifted to a smirk.

"How did *you* see that?"

"Just assume I never really left you alone." He took my bloody hand, pullin me down the hall.

"Is that why there's like, two drops of blood on you?" Blue interjected.

"No, there's only two drops of blood on me because I don't always make a mess."

"Is it done already?" I asked.

"No, but there's somethin you need to see."

Chapter Twenty-Two

Arlen

I was thoroughly confused.

In what would have been the food hall, there seemed to be a standoff. At the center of it was Noah, Vance, and Vitus uncle, Rex; all with guns held to their heads by their own people.

Vitus stood behind them like he was a crowned prince. A man with darker features was right beside him.

Acolytes, too many to count, stood by every exit. Coming through a cellular's speaker was Romero's voice, soundin rather smug.

Cobra and Katya stood off to one side, both lookin like they'd dove in tomato soup, Kat still looked prim and proper, despite that, although, her face was serious for once, as was Cobra's.

I refused to cower into Grimm when Vitus looked right at me, a smile lightin up his face. Bile rose in my throat at the sight of these men, but that's all it was. They made me sick, made me hate, and they'd hurt me, but they didn't fuckin scare me.

Blue stepped closer to me as an act of silent support. Vitus's eyes shifted to her. The immediate curiosity I saw there had me pushin her behind me.

Grimm squeezed my hand, bringin me closer to his side and helpin me block her.

"You have two minutes to tell me something I want to hear before everyone in that room tears you a new asshole." Romero's voice filled the silence.

It was odd not to see him front and center; it only solidified how he felt about Cali that he wouldn't leave her side while she was carryin his lil spawn.

"I want to meet you face to face. I'll come to where you are, and, as an act of faith you can have my father, my uncle, and Noah. I was gonna toss my cousin in too, but I'm told he's dead." He winked at me, the ballsy fuck.

This wasn't what I'd been expecting him to say at all. I couldn't even play the, *but they're his family* card. Family wasn't defined by blood. I was walkin proof of that. Mine stood around me, half wearin satanic masks.

"He has leverage," Grimm said quietly.

"Continue," Romero commanded with no change in his vocal inflection.

"I just need a week. I'll meet you face to face and then we go from there."

"You haven't told me why the fuck I wouldn't just kill you now and still get what I want."

"Well, you could've killed me the second I became a problem. But you didn't. You've been waiting for me to show my cards. *That's* why you take these fuck-ups off my hands and meet me in a week. We can iron out the details later of why later."

The room went so silent you could hear a pin drop.

"He's gonna take the deal," I mumbled, a split second before he did exactly that.

"One week. I'll get a hold of you, not the other way around." The line went dead.

"What just happened?" Blue asked from behind me.

I didn't fuckin know, and at that moment, I didn't care. Four of the men I'd came for would be dead. Three were right in front of me, comin back to my home turf. Four out of five was pretty damn good odds. I didn't care how they got there. I wanted them so badly I was nearly salivating at the mouth.

Vance's eyes locked with mine and I think he got the message clearly.

His ass was mine. Literally.

Chapter Twenty-Three

Arlen

We rode in the backseat this time.

For the first few hours we exchanged theories on what the hell kinda information Vitus could possibly have that made him feel so invincible.

"Vitus is naturally going to take his father's place. If you want to live out here, there's one man you don't make an enemy of. Sure as shit what his dad did," Cobra vented.

I'd worked that out already. I was on to more pressin matters.

Like the fact that my muscles were feelin my warrior moves from a bit ago, that I'd just faced the men who'd put me in this position in the first place, and how *badly* I wanted Grimm right then.

Our prisoners were bein transported in the back of a large, windowless van between two SUVs. I stared out the window at the black sky for a minute before adjusting my head in Grimm's lap.

He was replying to Cobra when I reached for his zipper. I worked it down, and adjusted again so I could slide my hand down his pants. His cock was already hard, clearly, he felt how I did. We just wanted to kill and fuck. Nothin was wrong with that.

He was solid and warm in my hand. He lifted slightly, allowin me to free him. His erection stood tall and proud in the darkness of the backseat. I encircled it, rubbing a throbbing vein with my thumb.

It was so smooth.

He grabbed a fistful of my hair, forcibly guiding my mouth down onto his cock, making me take him all.

I fought not to gag as the head hit the back of my throat. Grippin him with my hands, I lay on my side and started sucking him hard.

This I'd done quite a few times before. I knew how to cup his balls, swirl the tip of my tongue around his silky tip, and deep throat him back to back.

During a small lapse in silence, I was certain the suction noise echoed around the car. Knowin they heard me had my blood crusted thighs clenchin together.

I worked him harder, moanin in delight at the first taste of his pre-come. He scooped up some of the saliva running down my face, and then slid his hands down the back of my shorts, using it to lube between my cheeks before easin two fingers inside my puckered hole. The burn was delicious.

As he finger-fucked my ass, I eagerly sucked his dick.

I was a whore, greedy for his come to spray across my tongue as our friends sat in the front seat. My breathin became impossible to control. I wondered if I could get off with his thumb working my rim.

Poppin his cock out of my mouth, I turned my cheek into his lap, licking his plushy sack before gently easin his right nut between my lips, then the left, paying them equal attention.

I felt his abdominal muscles tightening, and heard him tell Cobra to watch the road, a breathy laugh following.

"Put my dick in your mouth," he gruffly commanded, turning me onto my stomach.

I did as he said, easily slipping his saliva drenched member back where it belonged. He took hold of my hair again, and proceeded to savagely fuck my face, driving his fingers in and out of my ass at the same tempo.

"That's it, good girl," he praised.

When he twitched, I was ready. He didn't warn me, didn't even have to force me lower.

"Goddamn, Brat. Fuck," he cursed softly, grippin my hair so hard my eyes stung.

I happily deep throated as he came, milkin his balls so I got every drop, feelin the tangy liquid slide down my throat.

After a complimentary twirl around his tip, I tucked his cock away before lying on my back again. I knew my face was a wet mess, just like my eyes were watering from his grip on my hair and makin myself not gag; I smiled up at him anyway.

"We'll be home in less than ten," he said. Due to the fact he wasn't touchin me, I knew what that meant. The word 'home' made my heart swell. *Home* was with him. *Home* was with our family.

Home was where Vance would soon find out how great it felt to be fucked in the ass without givin permission.

"Why did Romero cut the mayor off?" I asked to distract myself from the inferno goin on inside me, licking the roof of my mouth for any trace of his semen.

"*Cabrona*." Katya tisked, making me grin.

"Sorry about that," I volunteered, not really sorry at all. I wondered if I should be worried that I didn't care *that* much, but then I'd *have* to care for it to be an option.

"No the fuck you're not," Cobra laughed. "Girl, I could watch that spank bank material every day. You two are hot together. There's nothing wrong with being sexual. It's human nature. We're animals after all, savages who figured out how to walk and talk."

"We agreed to just be friends, Kat. You can't say those things, now I'm in love," Cobra sighed dramatically, making Blue giggle. Bless her, she was so sweet.

Grimm took hold of my face, makin me give him my eyes before he answered, gently rubbin my cheek with the thumb that was just inside me. “We’re filthy,” I laughed.

“We’re the best kind of filth, Brat,” he smirked, pressin that same thumb to my lips for me to suck.

“You know Rome, so you know he isn’t one to be controlled. That’s what the mayor was doing. Romero found new suppliers outside Centriole. Now he won’t take any form of contact from him. There goes the mayor’s real power,” he finally answered, pulling his finger away.

“Makes….sense,” I cocked my head, furrowin my brows.

“What—.”

I reached up pressin my hand over his mouth to hush him, and he bit me.

“Ouch, you fucker.” I jerked away.

“Don’t fucking hush me.”

“Ya’ll are damn idiots, you know that? If the mayor wants to hold his power he needs the same thing Vitus needs to make nice with

Romero. And what better leverage is there than his 'daughter'? I'm best friends with the devil's fiancée, in love with the Grimm, and adore Cobra.

Romero's bitch of an ex could have easily told this to Noah, and, well, boom! I'm your leverage. Lock me away as a pawn. I reckon he didn't count on being ignored, so he brought in the Venom." The more I figured it out the faster I talked, and the more pissed I became.

All the people he'd sent outside the wall, the babies lost, the death of my real father. Using me, brainwashing Beth into what she had become. His offenses went on and on. He deserved to pay penance for his sins just like every other dick on my shit list would.

I began wonderin what it was the Venom would get out of this, especially now that Vitus had given up Vance?

What the fuck were all these people hiding?

Chapter Twenty-Four

Arlen

At three in the morning we arrived home.

The main gates manned by armed acolytes, swung open. Cobra drove the long distance to the main house, and parked in front of what I considered a mansion.

It was all so familiar, but like I was seein it for the first time. The main ceiling fixture was a black ram head in the center of an inverted pentacle that held four light fixtures.

The wall fixtures were deep golden colored ram heads serving as placeholders for candelabras in the shape of inverted crosses.

It was all comforting, somehow.

“Get ready,” Grimm laughed softly.

I was starin at the smooth hardwood floor when he said that; I didn’t see Cali until she rushed me. She grabbed my arm and hugged the hell out of it, and partially me.

I was so thrown off by her huggin me at all, I just stood there. “I missed you so much! I can’t hug you because my fucking stomach gets in the way.” Someone had clearly swapped my Cali with another. When did she like hugs?

I looked down and saw a perfect bump beneath a silk nightie. She wasn’t that big at all, though since she was normally the size of a toothpick, she probably did feel like a hippo.

“I missed you,” I said, quietly, trying to hold back tears and failing. Huggin her back, I felt a light sheen on her skin.

“Are you okay? You’re sweaty.”

She laughed and stepped back, right into a shirtless Romero.

His dark eyes flickered over me, and the fucker actually half-smiled. “Blood looks good on you. Welcome to the fam.”

I blinked. Was this real life?

Cali moved onto Grimm, inspecting him closely, then full on embracing Cobra, who lightly rocked her back and forth.

“This place wasn’t the same without you guys.” She smiled sheepishly, her blue eyes curiously stopping on Katya and Blue for a brief second.

She looked between me and Grimm and her smile grew. I had so much to tell her, and knowin I could tell her anything because she would understand it all better than anyone else. Seein the huge ruby on her ring finger, the bump, and overall aura she had, I knew she had her fair amount to tell me too.

But it was three in the morning.

I was dirty, she had obviously been busy, and Blue and Katya looked like they were about to fall asleep on their feet.

And then the acolytes came in.

We all moved out of the way as the Venom men, plus Noah, were dragged through the front door and towards the hall that led to the 'playroom', as the boys called it.

None of them were lucid, their heads lolled, feet limply following behind their hoisted bodies as they went past.

"Get them settled, and then meet me down here," Romero said, walkin Cali back towards the stairs.

Grimm wordlessly took my hand and did the same, keeping a few paces behind them.

"I wasn't done talking." Cali yawned.

"You guys need sleep," Romero replied as we branched off at the top of the stairs.

"Aw," I softly sighed when I realized he'd meant her and the baby.

Grimm shook his head at me, stopping at a black door, and pushin it open.

The smell of him hit me first, and I knew right then that this would be my favorite place to be. His huge blacked out tufted bed sat against a wall, neatly made up in silk linen and a plush lookin comforter.

The metallic dresser and armoire matched it perfectly. There was a closed door on each far wall. He sat me down on the cushioned ottoman bench at the foot of his bed, not bothering to turn on a light.

Kneelin, he pulled my socks and boots off my feet, and carried them off where they made a lil thunk on the hardwood floor. I dug my toes into the silky soft, faux fur rug under me. I leaned over; resting on my elbow with my chin in my hand, closing my eyes when a soft light spilled from what I assumed was his bathroom.

"Come on, Brat." He lifted me off the ottoman and practically carried me to the shower.

It took me way too long to realize he was ass naked. I felt the alluring steam and attempted to help him undress me.

"Why so tired all of a sudden?" I yawned.

"You're crashing from your sugar high."

"I haven't eaten any sugar."

He chuckled softly, placing me inside a glass shower with slate walls.

"It doesn't matter. You're home now, where you belong."

I nodded, leaning back against his chest, my front facing the opposite direction. The hot water felt *so* good.

"Was gonna run you a bath, but I can do that another day."

"That's sweet, Grimm," I smiled, pressin my cheeks back on his erection, making him laugh again.

"Must not be crashing too hard," he mused, gently parting my legs.

"Is that sausage?"

"You sound like me; haven't even opened your eyes yet and searching for food," Cali laughed.

That did the trick.

I squinted against sunlight, burrowing deeper into the amazing silk pillow. My body felt so languid. I smiled, still feelin the sensation of Grimm between my legs.

He'd been so sweet, so unlike his norm, washin me up after and tuckin me in. Ugh, I loved that man.

"I know that smile," Cali sighed wistfully.

Opening my eyes fully, I looked down the length of the bed to where she sat Indian style on the ottoman, bump facing me.

Her white-blonde hair was longer, pulled to the side in a fish-tail braid. She had on a halter dress that matched her eyes, lookin all soft and innocent—a damn lie.

"Hurry and get moving, we have breakfast to eat and people to torture."

"*We?*"

"I crashed last night after I got crashed." She laughed at her own joke, making me do the same. "Anyway, Rome , Cobe, and G, spent a long time in the playroom. Now, if you're a good girl and eat your cheerios, we get to play too."

I sat up, belatedly forgetting I was naked. I grabbed the sheet as Cali scoffed.

"Like I haven't seen those bean bags before."

"If mine are bean bags, yours are beach rings," I retorted, climbing out of bed.

"You got clothes in the closet," she told me, pointing to the other closed door.

I went to the door she'd pointed at and pulled it open, seeing Grimm had ensured I would have more than what I could possibly need. Everythin was nice and organized, his stuff on one side, mine on the other.

"Do you know what's goin on?" I asked her.

"Vitus now has six days. Rome got whatever he wanted from Noah and Vance, and Grimm may or may not have killed the other guy, not that I blame him. And *you* need to eat, so we can play. I haven't gotten to play in months, and now Noah is just in that room helpless and scared out of his mind."

I put on a pair of gray cargo pants, skippin underwear, pulled a comfy bra over my head, and grabbed a skin-tight black T and some socks. I put deodorant on, but that was it.

I could smell the scent of Grimm on my skin. I wasn't takin that away.

After a quick brush of my teeth and hair, I was ready for the day.

Cali said 'play'. I didn't want breakfast; I wanted blood.

"I want to rush in there and fuck them up on sight as badly as you do, but Rome taught me to go in slow, prolong the pain and make them feel it. They deserve every moment of their suffering. Plus, I am growing the future heir of the Badlands. I got to feed this kid a granola bar and some almond milk."

Heir? It hadn't really occurred to me the life she and Rome's kids were going to have. The life me Grimm's kid would have.

"You ain't worried?"

"Um, no." She side eyed me, understandin exactly what I was tryna say.

"My kid will be surrounded by a family of deviants. The devil's their father, death will be their cousin, and their uncle's a Savage."

"Grimm would be their uncle too."

"But your baby will be their cousin. You should get started soon so my son has someone to play with."

"It's a boy?!" I exclaimed, a lil too loudly as we entered the kitchen, secretly overjoyed at how acceptin she was of me bein with her brother. This was Cali though, one of the most open minded people I'd ever met, so it wasn't all that surprising.

"We don't know that for sure." Romero jumped in from where he stood, cutting up an apple, while Cora and Grimm leaned against the counter. "I don't give a fuck what they are, they're mine."

"See, how sweet he can be? He's going to be a good daddy," Cali quipped as Cobra pulled out a barstool for her, and then me.

My attention was pulled to the hot plate of food Grimm slid in front of me and the glass beside it. Rome sat down a saucer of apples, granola, and sausage patties in front of Cali who wasted no time digging in.

"You met the other two officially yet?" I asked her, spotting them out on the patio, lookin content.

"Blue is shy and real sweet. Katya is cool; I almost killed her for lookin at Romero like he didn't have any clothes on, but Cobra mediated. Plus, who can blame her? He's incredible."

Romero looked directly at her. "I told you I wouldn't fuck you till after lunch. Keep stroking my ego and soon your tongue will be stroking my—."

"Here, look at this," Grimm interrupted, sliding a small laminated book between our dishes.

I twisted my lips, taking a sip of what I found was the most amazing fuckin homemade lemonade on the planet, with *fresh* lemon, so I wouldn't laugh at the look on Grimm's face.

I focused on the lil book he'd just sat beside me.

"Leviathan cross of crucifixion, vise, garrote, hand-saw, tongue-puller, blow-torch, *seven* pairs of red tipped pliers, a fuckin *Cradle of Judah*?" I ticked off randomly. The book was at least ten pages long.

"Fucking great, isn't it?" Cobra asked, peering over our shoulders.

"They don't call it the devil's playground for no reason," Grimm added, liftin a strand of my hair to twirl around his finger.

"Where did you get a Cradle of Judah and a…he-ter-ricks fork?" Cali asked Romero.

"Babe, you know I can get whatever I want."

"Why are you showin us this?" I asked.

"Because you two will be putting on the show, so if you see something that's missing…." He let us fill in the blanks.

"What show?"

"My people want to watch, they get to watch. Plus it sends a message not to fuck with me again. Speaking of," he turned his dark ass gaze on me, "what do you want to do about Centriole?"

I sat there suddenly tongue tied, partially shaken that he was focusin on me directly. I didn't care how tough you thought you were; these three men were terrifying. I wasn't afraid of Grimm, cause I knew he'd never hurt me outside of our debauched fuckin.

Romero didn't have to say a single word. He had an aura about him. He was the owner of a medieval level torture room, enough said.

And Cobra , for all his jokes and sense of humor, it was clear he was fucked up too.

"What can I do? It's behind a stone wall," I finally responded.

"But if it wasn't?"

"I'd probably give everyone inside it a large dosage of reality." I shrugged.

"That's very…ominous."

"The elaborated version was draggin every civil leader into the middle of the street and slittin their throats cause, I know damn well they're aware of how they got their positions.

"I'd shove most of those rich pretentious fucks inside the revolting prison cells the mayor has outcasts locked away in for simply seekin refuge. And beyond that, put someone more competent in charge of them, and tear that hideous wall down."

"That's an excellent fucking answer." Romero grinned at me.

"If the wall comes down it's ours," Cobra cut in, his gaze shiftin to Katya and Blue as they joined us.

"That's the beauty of it all. Walls fall down." Rome smiled, one of those evil genius smiles when a grand scheme has come together.

"You're going to tear it down?" Cali asked, dunking her granola in milk.

"*We'll* be tearing it down," Grimm corrected. "No one's doing anything till Baby S is here. Can't just run at a wall and expect it to crumble. In the meantime…" he trailed off lookin at me expectantly.

"What else do you need, Brat?"

"A cattle prod." I was only semi-joking.

"We have three," Romero confirmed.

It was pretty damn luxurious for a torture chamber.

The tools were organized behind a chain-link fence that sectioned off the massive room.

The bigger ones were placed systematically about. There were plush couches and a damn bar in the far corner. I think what may have been a stripper pole at one time had been turned into a shackle bar, currently where Vance sat in nothin but his drawers.

Noah was stomach down on a long wooden table with some sort of device holdin his head in place.

Rex was most certainly dead. Half his bloodied body was submerged in a metal tub of what looked like leeches. The wet sounds emanating from it made me shudder.

Cali had swapped her blue dress for a shorter black one and some knee high boots. She looked like she was ready for a shoppin trip, not to kill someone.

I, on the other hand, was wearin my same outfit from earlier, and Katya, who had opted to join us, was dressed down.

Blue was positioned comfortably on the other side of the room, beside Cobra. She looked at him the way he looked at Katya.

"She has us," Cali said as if she'd just read my damn mind, struggling to pull a long metal contraption out of a chest.

"I think a good girl is what he needs," I shrugged, conscious of the fact I'd just said that in front of Kat. She didn't seem to care, which was really my point.

I wasn't tryna be a bitch, but I genuinely felt that way. Good girls could be bad, too. Regardless, Cobra deserved someone who would love all of him, lawd knows the man had issues that ran deep.

I turned and met Grimm's eyes from across the room, blowin him a kiss. He tried to fight a smile and lost. I completely melted. I felt him watchin me twenty-four-seven and I loved it. He moved away from the bar and began makin his way over to us, Romero followin.

"Whoever she is will be getting her ass kicked by both of us if she dares ruin that smile always on his face," Cali said, and looked right at Kat, provin she knew knew where my mind had been.

I scooted her out the way to get whatever she was struggling with, trying not to laugh. Her loyalty was iron-clad.

"I got it," Grimm said, coming up behind me and embarrassingly easily, pulling out what looked like an extended pair of forceps with rusted metal teeth. He raised his brows at me.

"Now, you know full well your sister is the one who wants to play with whatever that is."

"It's a tongue puller. Had you curious did it, Pixie?" Romero grinned, helping Cali from her crouched position.

"Are you ready?" he turned and asked me.

I looked through the chain links at Vance and Noah. I was beyond ready.

Chapter Twenty-Five

Arlen

Vance died first.

With a room full of acolytes and death by my side, it went flawlessly.

"Swap him with Noah," I said, returning the wicked grin Cali had given me.

This was half her idea, half mine. She deserved this as much as I did.

Without questioning our reasoning, Grimm unshackled Vance, leading him by the metal ring around his neck to the table Noah was shackled on.

Romero turned a lever in a circular motion, and the large metal panels resting against the top of Noah's head and jaw loosened.

"It's a vise," Grimm explained.

Romero dragged Noah off the table, and the man began to pray as soon as he his knees hit the ground.

"Not this shit again," he sighed.

Grimm shoved Vance down on the table in his place. He didn't make a sound, didn't even try to fight back as his arms were stretched above his head and secured in the ropes. Where was the fun in that?

Grimm spun the vise back shut, securing Vance's head in place.

I circled around to stand in front of him as Cali had Romero lift Noah off the floor.

"You're an ass man, right Vance?" I asked, stroking the hair on top of his head.

"Well, we know Noah is," Cali said, coming to stand by me.

We'd decided it would be best not to take unnecessary risks, and placed her where she couldn't possibly be hurt.

She held the position by Vance's head, and just like we wanted, Romero and Grimm easily lifted Noah up onto the table behind him.

Each held an arm as he struggled, and I dragged his boxers down, exposing his ugly blob of a dick. I ignored his cries, doing the same to Vance so his ass was exposed.

"You know what to do," Grimm said, dragging Noah's cock closer to Vance's ass.

"Please, show mercy," Noah mumbled, choking on a cry.

I started to laugh. Was he for real?

"This fucking pussy is not related to me," Romero snapped.

"Spread his ass," Grimm demanded, unabashedly grabbing Noah's cock, pulling on it like a rope.

Romero let his arm go and gripped Vance's cheeks, pulling them apart.

I moved out of the way, adjustin my grip on the prod Grimm had handed to me before we began.

"You hear that Brat? He asked for mercy." He smiled at me; force feeding Noah's cock into Vance's hole.

I smiled and lifted the prod, tappin the zapper once, twice.

The acolytes were shiftin about by this point in excited anticipation. As soon as Noah's tip touched center, Vance reacted, yellin out all kinds of obscenities. "Here honey, you're going to want to bite down."

I looked at Noah's face, how the tears leaked off it, the slobber as he begged like a fuckin coward. I was disgusted. I saw myself in his place, pleading for it all to stop and he did nothin but watch.

He hurt me, and he'd hurt my family countless times in the past.

I wanted him to *beg* for mercy, and then I'd give him death.

I jammed the prod up his ass and hit the button. He was forced to go balls in as his whole body convulsed forward.

Vance yelled, givin Cali the perfect opportunity to use her tongue puller. She clamped the device down and didn't let go, holding it in place even as he began to bleed.

"Move," I demanded, pullin the prod out and jamming it back in.

He screeched, gaggin as he jerked again. It took a good few minutes, and some leakage of crimson from his own hole, but he started to move. Noah thrust in and out so slowly I began to get bored.

Without warning I shoved him, removing his blood tinged cock from Vance's bright cherry asshole. He fell onto the stone floor with a loud thud; before he could even think about recovering, I placed the prod on the tip of his dick and hit the button.

"You could have done better than that shameful performance Noah, I remember," Cali callously stated.

Romero blinked, slowly, as if he'd just been switched on.

"Maybe he knows he can't compete with Vance," I shrugged.

"Fuck this," Romero mumbled at the same time Grimm physically moved me out of his way, pickin me up and placin me by Cali.

"Pull out Lilith!" Romero demanded.

"Good fucking choice," Grimm affirmed.

Me and Cali shared a look, neither knowin what they were talkin about.

Romero grabbed Noah by the leg and began dragging him across the room.

Cali let her forceps loosen when Grimm stepped up to the vise. "Watch," was all he said before he began turning the balled lever.

I moved closer, watchin the two iron planes inch together, compressing what was in their way—which happened to be Vance's head.

Grimm's muscles slightly tensed as he continued turnin the lever.

None of us paid any mind to Vance's screams. He kicked his legs, shiftin his bloody ass back and forth, struggling in his restraints. I knew it hurt, knew he felt the non-stop pressure on his bones as they prepared for a farewell crunch. The more he hurt, the better.

The bottom jaw cracked first. Teeth cracked and crumbled. His life ended when the top of his skull fractured, and out came pouring pieces of his brain in a mass of cerebrospinal fluid and golden red liquid.

"This thing is sick." Cali grinned, runnin her fingers along the top of the vise.

Lookin at the way his face had permanently contorted, I felt, like I'd done some vigilante justice.

Grimm stepped back, no emotion on his face whatsoever. He took my hand, and led me across the room to where Romero was.

Cali quickly followed, leaving her forceps on Vance's back.

Romero's steel toed boot was restin squarely on Noah's back so he couldn't go anywhere. Cobra looked like he was about to burst with glee so I knew whatever was bein dragged from behind the fence was some fucked up piece of equipment.

I was certainly correct.

"What the hell is that thing?" I asked Grimm.

"It's our version of a Nuremberg virgin, obviously with Lilith on top."

Was I expected to know what that was?

He positioned me in front of him, wrappin his arms around my middle. I snuggled myself into his embrace, kissin his cheek. We watched the acolytes get to work.

Whatever they had dragged out, looked like a giant wooden mummy tomb dotted with round holes. Some were open, some were covered.

When Cobra did the honors of opening the two wooden doors like one would a cabinet, I saw it was affixed with long iron spikes on both the doors and the back wall.

“Rome, you’ve been holdin out on me,” Cali pouted.

“No, you just never asked what was in here. Bet your ass memorizes that book now.” He glanced back at her with a smirk.

“Get him inside,” he said to two acolytes, steppin back to wrap his arm around Cali’s waist. I tracked his thumb gently massaging her bump and smiled.

“You know, you may be an asshole of epic proportions, per Cali’s usual words, only bein bested by Grimm when’s he’s a broody dick, but you ain’t that bad. *And* you care about the elderly.”

“I don’t brood,” Grimm said, squeezin my side.

“Well, you may be annoying as fuck, and a chick I only kept around for Cali’s sake— and Grimm’s, because he went soft on me—but I’m glad you’re home. But don’t tell anyone about the old folk. I got a rep to obtain,” he joked.

“That was so adorable I have tears,” Cali laughed, wiping wetness from her eyes.

“You have tears because you’re an emotional bitch, babe.”

He really just undid all progress with that sentence, but Cali just laughed it off and elbowed him.

We watched Noah loaded into the ‘Lilith’, and he fought for once, as best he could under the circumstances.

Grimm kissed my neck, and then rested his chin on my shoulder, speakin lowly into my ear.

“It was built to replicate the real thing. Those spikes won’t hit any vital organs.

He'll feel ten stabs through his flesh all at the same time." As he explained, Cobra slammed the doors shut.

The thick padlocked hinges interlocked, and the room erupted in cheers a second after a piercing cry that sounded more animal than man pierced the air.

Grimm placed another light kiss just beneath my ear, nippin the lower lobe before he spoke again. "Two spikes in the shoulder, two in the lower back, and one in each ass cheek."

He shifted, pullin me further back into him; I could his hardened cock through the fabric of our pants. "Three spikes in the chest, and one in the stomach. Do you hear the way he's screaming? The spikes are binding with each bloody wound. Listen to him struggle, making them go deeper.

"That closed in space, nowhere to go and only darkness to see. It only exacerbates the pain and misery."

I gripped his hands firmly in mine. This was a whole new form of dirty talk.

Cobra opened the doors, revealin a flash of Noah's bloody body, tearin the spikes free, just to slam them shut again, bringin forth another loud yell, this time, seeming to echo through the entire house.

Blood poured from the bottom of the Lilith and leaked from the open holes. But he wasn't dead yet, beneath all the chanting you could hear him moanin in pain.

His death wasn't meant to come fast. He was meant to suffer in agony, just like the Mayor of Centriole would.

"Take it to the Leviathan. We'll burn him sometime tomorrow," Romero ordered, nearly draggin Cali out the room.

"Come on," Grimm said, leading me after them.

We weaved in and out of the gathered in the house. *Ava satanas*, and *memento mori*, reached my ears more than once.

"What does *Memento mori* mean?" I asked as soon as we made it to his room without incident.

"Remember death," he answered, watching me kick my shoes off and shimmy my pants down. "They celebrate death as much as they do the devil."

I lifted my shirt off, droppin it to the floor. I stepped back to get a good look at him as he removed his own clothes.

"They celebrate me finding you." He closed the gap I created and clasped my hips, easily lifting me up onto his dresser. The metallic metal cooled my ass cheeks.

"I ain't nothin to celebrate," I laughed.

He cupped my face a lil harder than was necessary, ensuring he had my full attention. "You're the only woman I would get down on my knees and bow to."

"Grimm—."

He shut me up with his mouth on mine, tearin the fabric of my underwear as he removed them.

"You said you didn't need those words Brat, but you deserve them, and you only deserved to hear them if I meant that shit." He pulled back, makin sure he had my eyes. "And I do. Whatever version of yourself you want to be. I'm going to love the fuck out of you, always."

"You're gonna make me cry," I mumbled.

"Think I already did," he smiled, slowly lickin the tears from my cheeks. "Do I need to make it better?" he teased, unclasping my bra.

I cupped his face, pressin a light kiss on the tip of his nose. "I love you Grimm, needed to remind you of that, and yes, I think I'm owed some sex. *After* you tell me how Noah's goin to die in that box."

He pulled his cock out and brought me closer, wrapping my legs around his waist.

I knew he could feel how wet I was for him. I felt it on my thighs. He positioned one hand a little above my head on the mirror attached to the dresser, and grasped my thigh with the other.

"He's either dead already, or, the more likely option," he slowly pushed inside me, capturing my low groan in his mouth. "He's going to drown in his own blood as it fills up his lungs."

He began to fuck me, biting down hard on my shoulder. I grasped that perfect, toned ass of his beggin him to go deeper.

Liftin his hand, he grabbed my neck, and slammed me backward, never losing his momentum. Somethin fell off the dresser, breaking as it hit the floor.

I heard the mirror crack, and slowly splinter due to the force of our bodies movin together. The first shard fell soon after.

"Ow," I hissed, feelin an exposed edge dig into my skin.

I instinctively moved forward, but Grimm shoved me back, holding me in place.

"Grimm—." I began, feelin the blood trickle down my flesh.

He grabbed my wrists tightly, stretching them above my head, pinning them to the broken mirror before saying, "Shut the fuck up and take it."

The deviant, savage look in his eyes had me doin just that.

He drove in and out of me relentlessly, stretching me, destroying me. The louder I cried out, the harder he fucked me. He didn't slowly take me to the edge; he shoved me over it again, and again.

I came so much my eyes leaked tears. There was no relief, just steady constant tension and my pussy contracting around him. The pleasure shredded me.

I began struggling to catch my breath.

He lifted me up and carried me to bed, droppin me down bloody back in all, ridin my body the rest of the night.

Chapter Twenty-Six

Arlen

The remaining days leading up to the meeting were perfect; the day of the meetin things kinda went to shit.

The damn thing only lasted maybe twenty minutes. Five of those were spent in silence, ten roughly in shock; the other ten were brief negations and high emotions.

Vitus arrived punctually, eleven in the morning, to be exact.

He wasn't the problem, though. Well, he was but not in the way I would've thought.

He came with information and a confidence.

I sat beside Grimm in the dining room, our delegated meetin spot. Cali was beside me, and Romero was at the head of the table.

Acolytes stood on the offense and defense, watching for the slightest hint of a threat from him or any of the four men he'd brought along.

By the smile on his face I should've known this wasn't going to be a great conversation.

"I gave you three men and didn't ask for anything in return. All I'm asking for now is an alliance."

The silence after that stretched for a full five minutes.

"Why the fuck would I form an alliance with you?"

"Because I'm going to go out on a limb and say you want to destroy Centriole as badly as I do. And I don't want any part of your empire. I just want an alliance with it."

"Keep going," Cali said, waving her hand in the air.

"There's not much to it. They have someone inside the prison I want back."

Romero laughed, scrubbing a hand over his face. "Are you shitting me? Did you think I'd help you out of the kindness of my heart?"

"No, but if you really do consider these lovely people at this table your family, you'll do it for your niece or nephew."

I shifted; Grimm reached over and took my hand. Sittin here staring at Vitus smiling fuckin face made me feel as if daddy long legs were all over my skin.

"You're not making much sense, Vitus. Spit it, out or get the fuck out of my house." Romero stood up, clearly ready to be done with this.

"See, that's why I like you, Romero. You're a take no shit kinda guy. I have a few planters inside that can help us when you accept my alliance.

"We had Beth with us, and came to find out," he leaned back dramatically, "she was pregnant, by Cobra. And if one of you wants to dispute that, it's understandable. But she said he was the last man to touch her before we got her. My dad was going to use the kid as leverage himself when the mayor didn't come through with his end of their deal.

"She ran away, got herself caught up with some people who knew some people and, you can guess why her being back inside Centriole would be relevant to any of you."

What. The. Fuck?

No one said a word. I thought the bitch was dead, and now here she may be pregnant with my niece or nephew? By fuckin Cobra, of all people? *Our* Cobra.?

"If any of that is remotely true—that's a real huge *if* by the way—then why was he hunting down Arlen?" Cali asked, not missing a beat.

"Well, probably because he doesn't believe Cobra would care enough about his kid to claim it. And then, he'd still need leverage."

"We all know he isn't going to let a little savage from the Badlands knowingly grow up in his precious city, especially if his daddy is a heathen.

"Don't believe me, tell me go fuck myself. All you need is a simple DNA test. Actually," Vitus hummed thoughtfully, "*that* right there is our leverage against him. Keep him happy and out of our hair for a little while. If you think that's *all* I know, it isn't. But I have to have some leverage of my own. *Just* in case." He stared dead straight at Romero, and I got the inkling that wasn't all for show.

What the fuck else could there be outside of that? Goddamn Romero in all his secrecy. I glanced around when no one said anything.

Cobra had a completely unreadable expression on his face, and Grimm looked slightly irritated.

None of them were surprised my sister could be carryin his kid. To be frank, neither was I. I just didn't want to imagine the conception.

"What do you want?" Romero finally asked.

"I don't—."

"What the fuck do you want; only a dumbass would walk out of here without securing a guarantee."

Vitus waited a beat, then another.

"Give me the girl with the blue hair."

What?

"Fuck that," Cali said at the same time Romero said, "Done."

"You can't fucking do that Rome!" Cali yelled, pushing back from the table.

"I have to."

"What does that even mean?" I snapped.

"We can't just send her with him, Rome." Cobra interjected, runnin a hand through his hair.

Romero ignored that at first, walking into the kitchen. “You don’t pick pussy over your fucking kid. We both know how high the chances are of the little shit being yours.”

“Why the hell do you care, anyway? You specifically told me you didn’t want Blue.”

Course, it was at that moment Blue herself was dragged down the stairs, Katya right behind her.

She was like an open book. She looked hurt, a little pissed, and then she saw Vitus and seemed to fit the pieces of what was going on together.

“What is happening?” Katya asked, placing a protective arm around Blue, just to be pulled away by an acolyte.

“Blue is going to spend some time with Vitus,” Romero replied.

At his words Blue immediately took a step back, but the acolytes prevented her from going anywhere.

"Please don't make me do this," she pleaded softly. Her struggle played out on her face when tears broke free.

I think my heart broke more because she didn't try to fight. She accepted her circumstance with a swallow and a tense nod.

Katya, on the other hand, was down on the floor like a damn wildcat, bein restrained by the acolytes and cryin and yellin curse words in her native tongue. But she was the only one.

It was calmly veiled chaos.

"I like you already," Vitus grinned victoriously when Blue took his hand.

Cali stood beside me, as helpless as I was. I think the saddest part of all this was, Romero was right. He *always* was.

"It's okay, I've been through this before," Blue told me on a near whisper, forcing a sad smile.

That didn't make it okay. That made it worse. I stepped forward to say somethin, but Grimm pulled me back.

"Wait," Romero said, walking towards them. He walked right up to Blue with something in his hand. By time any of us knew what it was, he was pressing it into the side of her neck. She cried out and instantly tried to jerk away. He was movin away again as fast as he'd gotten to her. A large red welt was now visible on her flesh.

"What the hell, man?" Vitus asked, actually lookin concerned.

"I just marked her. She's one of ours. I want her back *alive*."

"I'll be in touch," Vitus said, not looking pleased by that at all. He took her anyway, gently still. His men followed him out and that was it.

Romero held a hand up for silence. "Before any of you say anything else fucking stupid and insult my intelligence, Grimm seemed to be the only one that trusted me enough to know what I was doing. If you think

I was suddenly caught off guard you're as stupid as Vitus is." That was his fuck off speech I assumed.

He left too, taking Cali with him.

Cobra helped Katya up where the acolytes had left her and helped her back upstairs. If it weren't for the heaviness in the air, it'd almost be like all of it never happened.

Chapter Twenty-Seven

Arlen

He hadn't left his room in hours.

Katya was on the patio staring at the remains of Noah, which meant he was alone.

We walked down the hall, and paused outside his door. Cali found her balls before I could. She knocked twice, and then walked right in, leavin me to follow.

"Wow," I murmured, the second I entered "I forgot how different his room was from the rest."

"He likes color," Cali shrugged, making her way to his bed.

Cobra's room was done up in blues, yellows, and a dark green. It looked like somewhere someone royal would reside.

Hearin the shower water runnin, and unsure how long he would be, I followed Cali's lead.

Grimm and Romero had gone on some secretive as hell run an hour after Vitus left and had yet to return. The fact Cobra stayed behind let me know he was feelin some kind of way, which was to be expected, but he didn't have to do it alone.

I settled beside Cali on his bed, fluffing one of the gigantic pillows.

"Do you know how many come stains were lying in right now?" Cali asked, staring at the ceiling.

"For real? Ew, shut up," I laughed, playfully pushin her shoulder.

"Damn, I'm thinking I should stay home more often," Cobra said, walking into the room with nothing but a towel around his waist, and his red hair a shade darker from his shower.

Cali and I shared a quick glance with one another after focusing on his body longer than what was necessary.

Cobra wasn't as bulked up as Romero or Grimm, but he made up for it with toned definition and colored tattoos.

"Stop givin me those incestuous looks." He pretended to shield himself from us.

I rolled my eyes. "Put some damn drawers on, and then come sit with us," I sighed.

"We came for moral support. However you need it," Cali added.

Without responding to us he went to his dresser and retrieved some briefs. He respectfully added a layer of black sweats before crawling between us, smellin strongly of male bodywash.

The three of us sat with our backs against his headboard in absolute silence for a few minutes.

"Do you wanna talk about?" I asked, knowin Cali wouldn't.

He took my hand and then Cali's, just holdin them for comfort. It dawned on me the longer we sat without sayin a word; he was lonely too.

"I fucked up," he finally said.

"We all fuck up, Cobra, that's life," Cali replied, placing his hand on her bump.

"But I really fucked up. I might have a kid, and now Blue is…Romero knew," he finished, confusing me and Cali both.

He puffed his cheeks up, and then let out a noisy stream of air. His silver eyes stared off blankly into space as he got lost in whatever was goin on inside his head.

I had an inklin he liked Blue much more than he'd let on, because Cobra killed chicks left and right, and now she was with Vitus.

My stomach still coiled just thinkin of his name. Throw a potential baby by my scandalous bitch of a sister into the mix, and I couldn't imagine how the man felt.

Beth deserved everythin she had comin to her, in my opinion. We didn't have a full disclosure about everythin yet, but we would. And if this turned out to be true I'd be damned if I let the only untainted member of my family be used as a pawn in war.

"We've all been through the ringer Cobra. And if you do have a kid so what? You we won't let anything happen. Fuck Beth. We'll bring him or her home and that kid's going to have the best fucking life ever. You have to remember you aren't alone. Blue's going to be okay. You're going to be okay, too," Cali said.

I nodded my head, agreeing with her every word.

Romero and Cali had gone through hell.

Grimm and I had gone through hell.

Now, it was Cobra's turn.

Epilogue

Grimm

Did it seem like we would have trouble in paradise?

Sure as fuck did.

The Savages, though…

We're a family, blood or not, and every family goes through shit from time to time.

We were back on track a week later trying to figure out the best course of action. Vitus had been right.

The DNA test was the best option to get Frank, the mayor, to back the fuck off.

And so life went on.

My life, specifically.

I grinned up at Brat, and she smiled back.

She loosened her fatal grip on my hair, urging me to come higher.

Not bothering to wipe my face, I rose up and rested between her spread legs. I lightly trailed my fingers over the bruises on her neck.

She'd got her little ass shitfaced off hooch. If I thought Brat was a pain-slut sober, her drunk was a whole new fucking animal.

Last night was a special occasion. Brat took her initiation like a champ, rode me like a pro, goat blood and all, until I took over. My aching balls and happy dick agreed I'd made the right decision. I craved to make her pussy bleed.

"Tell me how happy I make you," I demanded.

She leaned up, licking her arousal clean off my face, beard and all. "You're gonna milk this forever aren't ya?" she asked with a laugh.

"I can't put into any more words how happy you've made me, Tell me how happy I make you."

"You just fed me some delicious pussy for breakfast, and let me put a ball and chain on your finger; I'm very fucking happy, Brat."

She grinned at her diamond, and looked up at me with full adoration. Every time she gave me her eyes, I loved her hellion ass a little more.

The most damaged parts of her soul still shone strong enough to give me a peace I'd never known. That fucking brimstone flaring inside her would forever be my altar to worship.

She was mercy. I was death.

She'd always be Sally. I'd be her Jack.

A goddess like Persephone, to a Dark lord like Hades.

Queen of death.

Queen of me.

For always.

Arlen

Death came to me in the form of a man.

He replaced the halo that had fallen from my head with a crown forged of bone, blood, and desert roses.

He gave me life, but didn't know it yet.

Looking back at the path I'd walked, I couldn't believe the woman I'd become, but she was someone I could be proud of. This whole journey was like watching a movie on the big screen.

I sat on the couch with Cali and Katya, relaxing for the final weeks before our lives turned chaotic again.

Across the room, stood a man straight out of the darkest of nightmares, and in his arms was a small bundle wrapped in pink. She was our key source of happiness it seemed, a temporary stress reliever to hold onto for a few moments.

He looked up at me with joy in his eyes as he gently handed her to Cobra. Romero, the bulldog of a dad he was, stood hovering over their shoulders'.

I wasn't sure of the precise moment this gorgeous man had come to mean *so* much to me. I think he had had me at the first choke-hold. It just took some time to get the wind in our sails.

He was an angry gray cloud, hovering over my head, just out of a reach. And then the drizzle started, but I didn't think much of it, because a little rain wasn't that big a deal.

Before I knew it, he was a thunderstorm that was rapidly becoming something more.

He was as lethal to me as he was alluring—He was my Tartarus hurricane.

I don't know what gave him the right to sweep in and wreak havoc on my fuckin soul, but I was so glad he had, because he'd destroyed me in the most beautiful way possible.

He showed me how beautiful hell could be and all the wicked delight to be found in the dark. What seemed like a tragedy at first, wound up being a blessing in disguise.

In this world, I was forced to change, enter uncharted territory to find my true strength and authentic self.

What survived may not be kind, but it was me. As my eyes came to rest on Cobra, I knew that for the best.

It was going to take a helluva lot of bloodshed to make this right.

I had a feelin in the pit of my stomach that his journey would be the one that pushed all of us to the breaking point, and exposed everything.

We would win the war, but there was no guarantee we would all be amongst the living when it was over.

Bonus Epilogue

Romero

I had an empire.

I had my own personal hell right outside my door.

I had an army at my beck and call ready to annihilate anyone who fucked with me.

I had two brothers, a family that would do *anything* for me.

None of that shit mattered.

It couldn't touch what was right in front of me.

My beautiful, dark fucking queen was the best thing that ever happened to me. In her arms was my best motherfucking achievement.

Adelaide Deville came into this world six days early, on the sixth day of May, at six sixteen in the morning. Her hair was dark blonde, her eyes still newborn blue. She was quiet and calculating, already as beautiful as her mother and as lethal as her father.

There may have been an accident where the doctor ended up dead, but Uncle Cobra and a nurse got her out just fine while Arlen stood by as doula.

It was almost as if she was aware we were a week away from going to war, and needed to be present right fucking now.

Cali knew I was standing in the doorway, just watching the two of them, probably thinking I was there to collect my extra limb. She'd just finished feeding, now fast asleep on her chest.

Her hypnotic blue eyes met mine, and she smiled.

She still looked at me like I was the only man in the fucking universe, and she was still everything to me.

"You know you got this," she said as I finally approached our bed.

"No, Pixie, *we* got this."

Bloodshed is what we did, but she *was* right.

No one came to the devil's playground and beat him at his own game.

COMING 2018

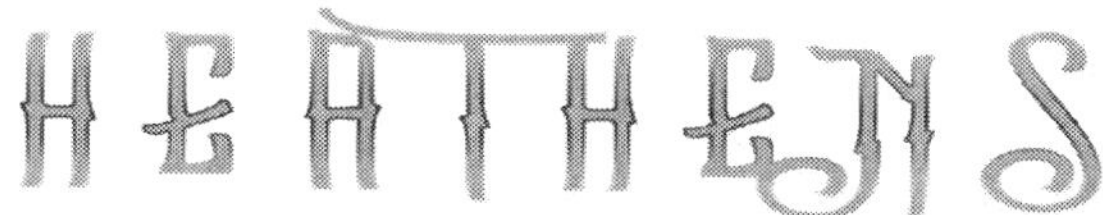

Add to TBR

Pre-order/Release Notification

Reader's Group

Playlist

Spotify

Gin Wigamore- Black Sheep

NF-10 Feet Down

NF-Mansion

BHM-Can You Feel My Heart?

Trevor Moran-Sinner

Coldplay- Fix You

Lacey Strum-Rot

The Neighborhood-Heaven

Disturbed-Down With The Sickness

5FDP-The Devil's Own

The Fray- Never Say Never

Stone Sour- Song #3

Tove Lo- Moments

Halestorm- The Reckoning

Fall Out Boy- Bishops Knife Trick

Three Days Grace- The High Road

Three Days Grace-Painkiller

Three Days Grace- Animal I Have Become

Wasteland- 10 Years

Outcasts

Evanescence- Imperfection

Shinedown- Cut The Cord

Sam Smith- Life Support

Niykee Heaton-Lullaby

Halsey-Gasoline

Halsey-Roman Holiday

PVRIS-Separate

PVRIS-Fire

The Weekend-Pray For Me

Breaking Benjamin-Red Cold River

Breaking Benjamin-Save Yourself

Breaking Benjamin-The Dark Of You

In This Moment-Sick Like Me

In This Moment-Forever

Want to be the first to hear about new releases or sales? Join my newsletter.

Sign Up Here

Follow me on: Facebook

Follow me on: Instagram

Upcoming Books 2018

King Of Hearts-6.09

Ace Of Spades-6.22

Heathens-TBA

Fuck Toy-7.01

Devils With Halos-TBA

Other books by Natalie Bennett

UltraViolence Duet

UltraViolence

Blue Velvet

Obscene Trilogy

Love Obscene

Love Corrupted

Love Depraved–10/31

Badlands Series

Savages

Deviants

Outcasts

Heathens

Degenerates *The next generation*

Standalones

Mercy: A Dark Erotica

Rose De Muerte

Pernicious Red

Fuck Toy

Acknowledgements

Evelyn Summers-Thank you for taking my words and making them 10x better. You have the patience of a saint. LOL

Michelle Brown- Everyone needs a PA like you.

Quib-This space will never be big enough for me to type out how much I appreciate you. Thank you for being my partner every single day.

Ena & Amanda- I've been using Enticing Journey for almost a year now, and I can't imagine doing a release without you guys. Thank you for everything that you do for your authors.

Bloggers- I appreciate all that you do. All the sharing, reviewing, and teasers, you are invaluable to any author.

Daqri Bernardo-You slay my covers every time with minimal instruction.

My Readers- Last but never least, thank every single one of you.

Outcasts

From the ones that have followed me on this learning path to the ones willing taking a chance on me for the first time.

You make this all worth it on the days I feel low. I promise to always do my best and put out the best work that I can.

Made in the USA
Lexington, KY
17 May 2018